THE WHOLEFOOD
COOKERY BOOK

By the same author:

COOKING AND CATERING THE WHOLEFOOD WAY

THE WHOLEFOOD COOKERY BOOK

URSULA M. CAVANAGH

Foreword by
Yehudi Menuhin

FABER AND FABER
London

First published in 1971
by Faber and Faber Limited
3 Queen Square London WC1
First published in this edition 1974
Printed in Great Britain by
Whitstable Litho Whitstable Kent
All rights reserved

ISBN 0 571 10617 X (Faber Paper Covered Editions)
ISBN 0 571 08871 6 (Hard bound Edition)

FOREWORD

Now, with this excellent and thorough cookery book, there is no longer any excuse to deny so many people in our civilized world the diet which has been so successful in my own experience at the Yehudi Menuhin School. So appetizing, wholesome and delicious a diet should not be denied one's family, oneself, one's clients, employees, patients, or even one's bosses!

Too long have we followed the fashion of 'convenience'—buying not really what we might choose, so much as what the supermarket, the food embalmers and the distribution systems wished to get rid of upon their too trusting and gullible shoppers. We are being persuaded that for our 'convenience' we must buy devitalized, harmful and often poisonous food, because it is processed, or packaged, improved, beautified, or treated to resist old age, and decay—in other words, we are not told anything about the food itself, but only about what the food has been subjected to from birth to death, what it has withstood at the hands of so many who have not even touched it. We learn nothing of the many thousand makers of chemicals, fertilizers, colourings, preservatives, bleaches, plastics, refrigerators and transport who have profited from that poor blanched asparagus tip long before you, the buyer, will have released it from its tin or plastic prison. How could it be otherwise? No one, no living thing, will have benefited from it *after* consumption, not even really the poor overworked doctors and nurses in our crowded hospitals. We have simply not understood the price we are called upon to pay for this 'convenience' in terms of cancer, arthritis and sickness in general. As our criteria of food we have substituted false premises and the sense of sight for common sense and the senses of taste and smell.

May this book restore our rightful pleasures, our good sense and our health.

Yehudi Menuhin

5

CONTENTS

INTRODUCTION

THIS is a cookery book for the very large number of people who enjoy the flavour of naturally grown foods and who dislike having their food and drink devitalized by chemical additives and other processing.

My aim has been to give clear practical instructions for appetizing recipes—with the emphasis on 'wholefoods' such as compost grown stone-ground wholewheat flour, brown sugar, natural unpolished rice, free range eggs and plenty of fruit and vegetables, compost grown wherever possible. These ingredients are easily obtainable from the Health Food Stores now springing up all over the place and from some of the more enterprising supermarkets. Where, occasionally, in the interests of an especially delicious flavour, I have used ingredients which are not strictly 'whole' the purist will I hope substitute accordingly. The real purpose of my book is to bring to more and more people, at a time when the pollution of our environment is becoming a real problem, the tremendous benefits of a basically clean and crisp wholefood diet.

Wholefood cooking puts no extra strain on housewife or cook. So whether you are a beginner in this sphere or a convert wishing to cook more ambitiously, there are rewarding culinary experiences ahead. As Mr Yehudi Menuhin said in the Preface to my first book written for schools, hospitals, canteens etc., 'the proof is in the pudding'!

URSULA M. CAVANAGH

SUGGESTED ADDITIONS TO THE STORE CUPBOARD

100% compost grown stone-ground wholewheat flour
100% compost grown stone-ground wholewheat self-raising
  flour
Barbados sugar, Demerara sugar, Natural brown rice, Honey

Vegetable oil: Safflower, Sunflower, Olive or Corn
Apple cider vinegar, Sea salt

OVEN TEMPERATURES

Very Cool	225–250 °F.	or ¼–½	Gas Regulo (107–121 °C.)
Cool	275–300 °F.	or 1–2	Gas Regulo (135–149 °C.)
Warm	325 °F.	or 3	Gas Regulo (163 °C.)
Moderate	350 °F.	or 4	Gas Regulo (177 °C.)
Fairly Hot	375 °F.	or 5	Gas Regulo (190 °C.)
Fairly Hot	400 °F.	or 6	Gas Regulo (204 °C.)
Hot	425 °F.	or 7	Gas Regulo (218 °C.)
Very Hot	450 °F.	or 8	Gas Regulo (232 °C.)
Very Hot	475 °F.	or 9	Gas Regulo (260 °C.)

MEAT COOKING TIMES

Roasting

Beef and Lamb	20 minutes to the lb. and 20 minutes over
Veal and Pork	25 minutes to the lb. and 25 minutes over

Boiling

Bacon, Beef, Ham and Pork	25 minutes to the lb. and 25 minutes over
Poultry	30 minutes to the lb.

ABBREVIATIONS

The following abbreviations have been used throughout:
tbs.   = 1 level tablespoon

dsp.   = 1 level dessertspoon
teasp. = 1 level teaspoon

METRIC WEIGHTS AND MEASURES

Approximate Equivalents   *Exact Equivalent*

½ oz.	= 15 grams (g.)	
1 oz.	= 30 grams	28·3 grams
4 oz.	= 120 grams	
8 oz.	= 240 grams	
1 lb.	= 480 grams	453·6 grams
1 gill	= 1·5 decilitre (dl.)	
1 pint	= ½ litre (l.)	·568 litre
1¾ pints	= 1 litre	·994 litre
1 inch	= 2·5 cm.	2·54 cm.
6 inches	= 15 cm.	

All recipes in this book are for four people.

SALAD DRESSINGS

Throughout this book, wherever mayonnaise or french dressing are referred to, the following home-made recipes should be used:

Mayonnaise
2 egg yolks
2 dsp. apple cider vinegar
pinch sea salt, pepper, barbados sugar
¼ pint olive oil, safflower oil, corn oil or sunflower oil
Beat up the egg yolks with the apple cider vinegar in a liquidizer or with a hand whisk or fork. Add the sea salt, pepper and sugar. Pour in the oil steadily and continue quite fast beating all the time until the mixture is thick and creamy. Bottle and keep in a cool place until required.

French Dressing
4 tbs. apple cider vinegar

pinch of sea salt, pepper, barbados sugar
12 tbs. olive oil, safflower oil, corn oil or sunflower oil
Mix the vinegar and the seasonings and pour in the oil. Shake
well and bottle for use when required. The addition of $\frac{1}{4}$ teasp.
mixed herbs makes a pleasant change.

1-Starters

1. Melon
2. Hot Grapefruit
3. Pig's Liver Pâté
4. Calves' Liver Pâté
5. Chicken Liver Pâté
6. Veal and Beef Pâté
7. Mushroom Canapés
8. Chicken Canapés
9. Prawn Canapés
10. Prawn Cocktail
11. Hors-d'œuvre
12. Scampi with Sauce Tartare
13. Devilled Eggs
14. Poached Eggs in Aspic
15. Asparagus Eggs
16. Potted Shrimps
17. Prawns in Aspic
18. Smoked Salmon
19. Avocado Pears

1. Melon

1 melon, either cantaloup or
  water
1 orange
2 oz. glacé cherries

2 oz. powdered ginger
2 oz. demerara sugar
cocktail sticks

Cut melon into four slices. Cut the flesh from the skin and cut into strips across; replace the strips of flesh on the skin, pushing one strip forward and one strip backwards alternately. Peel and slice orange placing one slice of orange and one glacé cherry on cocktail stick and spearing on to the middle of each melon slice. Serve with powdered ginger and demerara sugar.

2. Hot Grapefruit

2 grapefruit
2 oz. glacé cherries

2 oz. demerara sugar
$\frac{1}{4}$ pint sherry

Cut and prepare grapefruit very thoroughly. Sprinkle with sugar and sherry; place one glacé cherry in the middle, and place in oven 350 °F. (Reg. 4) for 10 minutes before serving.

3. Pig's Liver Pâté

1 lb. belly of pork
$\frac{1}{4}$ lb. pig's liver
1 egg
$\frac{1}{2}$ oz. sea salt

$\frac{1}{2}$ teasp. black pepper
1 tbs. chopped parsley
$\frac{1}{2}$ tbs. plain wholewheat flour
1 grated onion

Mince pork and pig's liver finely, add the rest of the ingredients and mix well. Put mixture into mould or terrine, cover with thin streaky bacon and place in a pan of hot water. Cook in oven 375 °F. (Reg. 5) for $1\frac{1}{2}$ hours. Pour off surplus fat and cool with weight on top for 24 hours.

4. Calves' Liver Pâté

Béchamel sauce	¾ lb. calves' liver
½ pint milk	¼ lb. fat bacon
1 onion	1 tbs. lemon juice
2 cloves	1 clove garlic
4 peppercorns	2 tbs. mixed dried herbs
1 bay leaf	1 tbs. chopped parsley
1 blade of mace	sea salt, black pepper
1 oz. butter	1 egg
1 oz. plain wholewheat flour	4 rashers streaky bacon

Heat milk with onion stuck with cloves, the peppercorns, bay leaf and mace. Leave in warm place for ½ hour then strain. Melt butter in saucepan, stir in the flour and cook for a minute or two; add the flavoured milk, then leave sauce to cool.

Line terrine with streaky bacon. Mince liver and fat bacon, mix with other ingredients. then stir in the béchamel sauce and beat well. Turn into terrine, cover and place in pan of hot water. Cook in oven 350 °F. (Reg. 4) for 1½ hours. Cool with weight on top and leave for 24 hours or longer before using.

Serve in slices with melba toast.

5. Chicken Liver Pâté

1 onion	1 sprig thyme
1 oz. butter	1 bay leaf
1 clove garlic	sea salt, black pepper
½ lb. chicken livers	1 tbs. brandy
1 tbs. chopped parsley	

Chop onion, garlic and chicken liver; cook gently in the butter. Add herbs and seasoning, and cook for a further 5 minutes. When cold, mince or pound several times, stir in the butter from the pan and the brandy. Pack firmly into a mould or terrine, cool for 24 hours with weight on top.

6. Veal and Beef Pâté

½ lb. stewing steak
½ lb. stewing veal
1 oz. butter
2 oz. water
sea salt, black pepper

In muslin bag:
1 bay leaf
1 clove garlic
1 blade mace

Chop up meat, place in casserole with water, butter, herbs and seasonings, cover and cook in oven 300 °F. (Reg. 2) for 3 hours. Remove herbs and cool. Mince twice and place in small terrine. Cover with buttered paper and weight the top. Leave for 24 hours. When cold pour off excess liquid and cover with melted butter.

7. Mushroom Canapés

4 slices wholewheat bread
4 oz. mushrooms
½ pint milk or cream
1 oz. plain wholewheat flour

1 oz. butter
1 teasp. garlic salt
pepper

Cut bread into four large rounds with fluted cutter, toast on one side only and brush untoasted side with melted butter. Slice and cook the mushrooms gently in butter, add the flour to make a roux, add the cream or milk and stir until thick. Add seasoning and pile mixture on to the canapés.

8. Chicken Canapés

As mushroom canapés, using 4 oz. minced chicken.

9. Prawn Canapés

As mushroom canapés, using 4 oz. prawns.

10. Prawn Cocktail

½ pint prawns
½ cucumber
3 tbs. mayonnaise (see page 11)
1 tbs. tomato sauce

1 tbs. white wine
1 lemon
1 lettuce
salt
cayenne pepper

Cut cucumber into small, long-shaped wedges, place in bowl together with prawns. Mix mayonnaise, tomato sauce and white wine together and stir into prawn mixture. Season, and place on lettuce leaves in glass dishes garnished with lemon slices and cayenne pepper.

11. Hors-d'œuvre

2 small tins anchovies
4 eggs
4 tomatoes
4 oz. haricot beans (cooked)
2 sticks celery
1 bottle stuffed olives
2 oz. olive oil
2 oz. cider vinegar
2 small cooked beetroot
½ cucumber

2 carrots
1 lb. cooked potatoes
1 bottle gherkins
4 oz. mayonnaise (see page 11)
1 oz. butter
chopped parsley
chopped chives
cayenne pepper
sea salt and pepper

Anchovies   Sprinkle with chopped parsley, chives and cayenne pepper.

Stuffed Eggs   Hard boil the eggs, remove yolks, mash well and mix with butter, mayonnaise, salt and pepper. Return to cases.

Tomato Salad   Slice tomatoes thinly, sprinkle with oil, cider vinegar, salt, pepper and chives.

Haricot Beans   Mix with oil, cider vinegar, salt and pepper, sprinkle with parsley.

Beetroots   Dice and mix in oil and cider vinegar; sprinkle with chives and parsley.

Celery	Slice finely, mix with oil and cider vinegar, sprinkle with chives.
Cucumber	Slice thinly, sprinkle with cider vinegar and salt.
Carrots	Shred, toss in equal parts of mayonnaise and vinegar and oil.
Potato Salad	Dice, mix with mayonnaise, sprinkle with chives and parsley.
Olives	Slice.
Gherkins	Slice.

Serve Hors-d'œuvre in separate dishes or on individual plates.

12. Scampi with Sauce Tartare

6 oz. shelled scampi
1 packet wholemeal bread-crumbs
2 eggs

fat for frying
lemon slices
parsley

Egg and breadcrumb scampi twice and fry in deep fat until golden brown. Serve with Sauce Tartare, garnished with lemon and parsley.

Sauce Tartare:
½ teasp. salt, pepper, made mustard
1 dsp. cider vinegar

2 egg yolks
2 tbs. olive oil
1 teasp. chopped parsley, gherkins and capers

Mix salt, mustard and pepper with vinegar in small bowl. Add egg yolks and beat with wooden spoon. Gradually add oil until thick and smooth. Add parsley, gherkins and capers.

13. Devilled Eggs

4 hard-boiled eggs
2 teasp. Escoffier Sauce Diable

1 lettuce

Cut eggs in half lengthwise, remove yolks, mash well and mix with diable sauce. Return to cases and serve on lettuce leaves.

14. Poached Eggs in Aspic

4 eggs
2 oz. ham
2 oz. cooked peas
½ chicken bouillon cube

½ oz. gelatine
tarragon leaves to decorate
1 lettuce

Dissolve chicken cube and gelatine in hot water, leave to cool. Line four small dishes or moulds with peas and slivers of ham. Poach the eggs and place one in each dish. Cover with chicken jelly, and when set turn out on to lettuce leaves and decorate with tarragon leaves.

15. Asparagus Eggs

12 heads of asparagus
1 lb. spinach
2 oz. butter
3 drops lemon juice

3 eggs
2 tbs. milk
salt and pepper

Cook asparagus, chop and keep warm. Cook spinach, sieve, reheat in saucepan with 1 oz. of butter, lemon juice and seasonings. Beat the eggs and milk together and cook slowly in saucepan with remaining butter until it starts to thicken. Add the chopped asparagus and cook until quite thick. Place spinach on dish, pour over it the asparagus custard and serve with hot buttered toast.

16. Potted Shrimps

1 pint shrimps
3 oz. butter
salt
cayenne pepper

nutmeg
1 lemon
1 lettuce

Heat the butter and turn the shrimps in this until they are well coated. Add the seasonings, pour into small dishes or moulds and leave until the butter is set. Turn out on to lettuce leaves and garnish with lemon slices. Serve with cayenne pepper and melba toast.

17. Prawns in Aspic

1 pint packet aspic jelly
½ pint boiling water
5 tbs. thick mayonnaise (see page 11)
1 tbs. sherry

1 egg white
12 oz. shelled prawns
salt
pepper
slices of tomato and cucumber

Make the jelly and leave it to half set, then mix in the sherry, mayonnaise, and stiffly beaten egg white, salt and pepper and, lastly, the shelled prawns. Pour into a well-oiled mould and leave to set. Turn out and decorate with cucumber and tomato slices.

18. Smoked Salmon

8 oz. smoked salmon

Slice thinly and serve with wedges of lemon and thin slices of brown bread and butter.

19. Avocado Pears

4 avocado pears
2 oz. olive oil

1 oz. cider vinegar
salt and pepper

Halve the pears, remove the stones and sprinkle with vinegar, oil and seasonings.

2-Soups

20. French Onion Soup
21. Cream of Onion Soup
22. Chicken Lemon Soup
23. Game Soup
24. Turkey Soup
25. Lentil Soup
26. Winter Noggin
27. Cucumber Soup
28. Tomato Soup
29. Gazpacho
30. Celery Soup
31. Walnut Soup
32. Party Nip
33. Green Pepper Soup
34. Fresh Pea Soup
35. Potato Soup
36. Bean Soup
37. Fish Soup
38. Beef Broth
39. Scotch Broth
40. Cream of Vegetable Soup

20. French Onion Soup

1 lb. onions
1 oz. butter
1¾ pints stock
sea salt and pepper

1 oz. wholewheat flour
2 oz. grated cheddar cheese
croutons of wholewheat bread

Cook sliced onions in the butter, in a pan with a tight-fitting lid, for 20 minutes very gently. Add 1½ pints of the stock, season well and allow to simmer for a further 30 minutes. Mix flour to a smooth paste with cold stock and add to the soup and cook for a further 10 minutes. Serve in large tureen with croutons and grated cheese on top.

21. Cream of Onion Soup

4 oz. sliced onions
1½ oz. butter
¾ oz. wholewheat flour
1½ pints of milk

2 tbs. cream
2 egg yolks
sea salt and pepper
croutons of wholewheat bread

Sauté sliced onions gently in the butter, then add the wholewheat flour and stir well for 2 or 3 minutes. Add the hot milk gradually, bring to the boil and simmer for 20 minutes. Remove from the heat, season well and add the cream and egg yolks beaten up together; reheat but do not boil. Serve with croutons of fried wholewheat bread.

22. Chicken Lemon Soup

2½ pints well-seasoned
   chicken stock
3 eggs

6 tbs. cooked natural brown
   rice
juice of one lemon
sea salt and pepper

Heat chicken stock to boiling point; remove from the heat and add the cooked rice. Beat eggs with lemon juice and then dilute with a little hot stock, stirring constantly, and when quite smooth pour into the soup and cook very gently for a few minutes; do not boil. Stir quickly so that the egg mixture gets thoroughly mixed in with the stock. Season well and serve.

23. Game Soup

The remains of grouse or any game	2 cloves
5 bacon rinds	sea salt and pepper
4 pieces of celery	1 tbs. chopped parsley
2 onions	2 tbs. sherry
2 carrots	croutons of wholewheat bread

Put all ingredients except parsley and sherry into a saucepan, cover with water and simmer slowly for 2 hours. Strain, reheat and add sherry and parsley. Serve with croutons of wholewheat bread.

24. Turkey Soup

1 turkey carcass	1 bouquet garni
3 carrots	sea salt and pepper
3 sticks celery	2 tbs. natural brown rice
3 sliced onions	2 tbs. sherry
3 sliced tomatoes	croutons of wholewheat bread
3 tbs. chopped parsley	

Cover carcass with cold water and cook slowly for 2 hours. Add chopped carrots, celery, onions and tomatoes, parsley, sea salt and pepper and the bouquet garni. Add any gravy or stuffing leftovers and 2 tbs. of natural brown rice. Simmer for another hour, remove bones and bouquet garni, add 2 tbs. sherry and serve with croutons of wholewheat bread.

25. Lentil Soup

1 pint lentils	$\frac{1}{4}$ pint double cream
1 large onion	2 teasp. Marmite or Bovril
3 sticks celery	1 quart water
2 sage leaves	sea salt and pepper

Wash the lentils, put them in a saucepan with the water and add the sliced onion, the chopped celery and the sage leaves. Simmer gently until the lentils are cooked then put them through a wire sieve or strainer. Beat the cream and savoury extract together and add to the soup, season to taste and gently reheat. Do not boil.

26. Winter Noggin

Some veal bones	1¾ pints water
¼ lb. shin of beef	1 oz. butter
¼ lb. onions	1 tbs. vegetable oil
¼ lb. leeks	1 dsp. barbados sugar
¼ lb. potatoes	1 tbs. mixed herbs
2 carrots	sea salt and pepper
1½ oz. wholewheat flour	1 wine glass sherry

Roast the veal bones at the top of a very hot oven for 20 minutes. Clean and chop the onions, leeks, potatoes, carrots and meat. Cook in oil and butter over a good heat, stirring frequently. Add the sugar and let the mixture brown a little. Add the flour and let it brown but not burn. Add the water gradually, letting it boil between additions. Add herbs, veal bones and seasoning and let soup simmer for 2 hours. Strain, add sherry and serve.

27. Cucumber Soup

1¼ pints stock	2 cucumbers
1 large sliced onion	chopped chives
2 oz. butter	¼ pint double cream
1 lb. peeled and diced potatoes	sea salt and pepper

Sauté sliced onion gently in the butter, then add the potatoes, then the stock. Season well and cook fairly fast for 20 minutes. Sieve. Grate the two unpeeled cucumbers into the soup, add the cream and reheat, but do not boil. Sprinkle with chopped chives and serve.

28. Tomato Soup

2 oz. ham
1 stick celery
1 small onion
1 carrot
1 oz. butter
¼ pint double cream

1½ lb. tomatoes
1 pint stock
¼ pint warm milk
½ oz. cornflour
sea salt and pepper
croutons of wholewheat bread

Dice the ham, slice the onion, celery and carrot and sauté gently in heavy saucepan in the butter. Add the tomatoes and the stock and cook for about ½ hour until the vegetables are tender. Rub through a sieve and add the warm milk. Thicken with the cornflour rubbed to a smooth paste with a little cold milk, season well, boil for a further 5 minutes then add the cream and serve with fried croutons of wholewheat bread.

29. Gazpacho

2 lb. tomatoes
2 green peppers
1 cucumber
3 cloves garlic
6 spring onions

sea salt and black pepper
2 tbs. apple cider vinegar
4 tbs. olive oil
½ pint chicken stock

Peel and slice the tomatoes, finely slice and de-seed the green peppers, chop the garlic and the spring onions using the green tops as well. Combine all the vegetables in a large bowl, season well, add the oil and vinegar and chill in the refrigerator for ½ hour. Add the stock and serve cold.

30. Celery Soup

1 head celery
1 lb. potatoes
1 onion
sea salt and pepper
a sprig of thyme

1 bay leaf
2 pints of water
1 tbs. chopped parsley
1 oz. butter

Put the chopped celery, peeled and diced potatoes, sliced onion, thyme, bay leaf, sea salt and pepper in a saucepan, add the water and cook for 1 hour. Sieve, add more water if necessary, season, bring to the boil, add butter and parsley and serve.

31. Walnut Soup

1 lb. walnuts	sea salt and black pepper
2 tbs. chopped parsley	¾ pint milk
2 tbs. olive oil	¾ pint stock

Shell the walnuts, drop them in boiling water and skin them. Pound the nuts to a pulp and place in a saucepan. Add the parsley, olive oil, sea salt and pepper and the milk. Bring to the boil, add the stock and simmer gently for ½ hour.

32. Party Nip

1 quart milk	⅓ pint whisky
1 orange	4 tbs. cream
1 tbs. barbados sugar	grated nutmeg

Wash the orange in hot water and peel very finely. Simmer the peel in the milk very gently for about 5 minutes, add the sugar and stir until dissolved but do not boil. Remove the peel, cool the milk a little, stir in the whisky and beat all together well. Pour into warmed glasses, float a tablespoonful of cream on top of each portion and sprinkle with a pinch of nutmeg.

33. Green Pepper Soup

1 large green pepper	1 lb. tomatoes
1 onion	2 pints stock
1 oz. butter	sea salt and pepper
1½ oz. wholewheat flour	2 teasp. lemon juice

De-seed and slice the pepper; keep a few finely sliced rings aside for a garnish. Slice the onion and fry both vegetables in

the butter until soft but not brown. Blend in the flour. Add
peeled and chopped tomatoes and the stock and simmer gently
for ½ hour. Sieve, season well, add the lemon juice and serve
garnished with green pepper rings.

34. Fresh Pea Soup

1½ lb. peas	1 gill thin cream
4 spring onions	sea salt and pepper
2 large lettuce leaves	pinch of barbados sugar
1 gill milk	

Put the shelled peas into a heavy pan with the sliced lettuce
leaves, onions, sugar and seasoning. Just cover the peas with
water and simmer until they are soft. Pour off the liquid and
put the vegetables through a sieve. Return the purée to the pan
and add 1 gill of the liquid the peas were cooked in, the milk
and the cream and heat gently.

35. Potato Soup

1 lb. potatoes	1¾ pints water
1 stick of celery	¼ pint milk
1 onion	sea salt and pepper
1 tbs. wholewheat flour	1 oz. butter

Wash and peel the vegetables, grate and put in pan. Cover
with water and simmer for 2 hours. Sieve. Mix flour to a
smooth paste with the cold milk, stir into the soup and boil for
10 minutes. Season well and add a knob of butter just before
serving.

36. Bean Soup

1 lb. butter beans	¼ teasp. nutmeg
sea salt and pepper	¾ pint chicken stock
1 clove garlic	1 tbs. chopped parsley

Soak butter beans overnight, then simmer for 1 hour or until cooked. Drain the beans and mash them with the seasonings and a little of the liquid they were cooked in. Heat the purée in a saucepan, gradually adding enough stock to make a thick soup. Serve very hot garnished with chopped parsley.

37. Fish Soup

1 quart fish stock	2 oz. wholewheat flour
1½ oz. butter	½ pint milk
sea salt and pepper	½ lb. fillet of cod, cooked

Melt the butter in a saucepan, add the flour then the milk gradually, stirring all the time; add the fish stock, season well, flake in the fish and boil for a few minutes.

38. Beef Broth

1 lb. shin of beef	1 onion
2 quarts water	1 carrot
½ turnip	sea salt and pepper
1 stick of celery	

Cut the meat into very small pieces, place in a casserole. Wash and shred the vegetables, put in the casserole with water, sea salt and pepper and put the lid on. Put in oven 350 °F. (Reg. 4) for 1 hour, then turn off oven and leave for a further 2 hours.

39. Scotch Broth

1 lb. neck of mutton	1 tbs. pearl barley
1 carrot	3 pints water
1 turnip	sea salt and pepper
1 onion	1 teasp. chopped parsley
1 potato	

Dice meat, put in pan, cover with water, bring to the boil and skim. Dice vegetables and add to the pan with the pearl barley. Simmer for 3 hours, season well and add the chopped parsley.

40. Cream of Vegetable Soup

1 carrot
1 turnip
1 onion
1 stick of celery
1¾ pints water

1 oz. butter
¼ pint milk
1 tbs. wholewheat flour
sea salt and pepper
1 tbs. chopped parsley

Dice vegetables, put into pan with butter, seasoning and water. Cover and simmer for 1½ hours. Sieve. Mix flour with cold milk and add to the soup, boil for 5 minutes, add a little chopped parsley and serve.

3-Fish Dishes

Cold
41. Fish Jelly
42. Fish Mousse
43. Fish Slaw
44. Fish and Rice Salad
45. Fish Mayonnaise
46. Lobster Creams
47. Lobster Soufflé
48. Salmon Relish
49. Salmon Mousse
50. Prawn Salad
51. Shrimp Mousse
52. Soused Herrings
53. Scrambled Fish

Hot
54. Fish Pancakes
55. Baked Fish Roll
56. Fish and Bacon Pie
57. Orange Plaice
58. French Fillets of Sole

59. Sole with Wine and Mushrooms
60. Salmon Trout
61. Chinese Cod Steaks
62. Chinese Scampi
63. Fried Scampi with Tartare Sauce
64. Baked Stuffed Haddock
65. Kedgeree
66. Haddock Omelette
67. Crab Pie
68. Crab Stew
69. Prawn Risotto
70. Prawn Curry
71. Creamed Prawns
72. Cheese Prawns
73. Lobster Newburg
74. Lobster Croquettes
75. Stuffed Herrings
76. Scallops

31

41. Fish Jelly

1½ lb. white fish
½ pint milk
¼ pint water
2 oz. natural rice
2 tomatoes
1 oz. margarine or butter

1 oz. plain wholewheat flour
¼ pint aspic jelly
sea salt, pepper
½ cucumber
1 bundle watercress

Simmer fish gently in salted milk and water. When cooked, remove skin and bones from fish and then flake. Keep the fish stock. Cook rice in boiling salted water for 20 minutes. Strain and add rice to fish. Melt butter or margarine and mix in flour. Add ½ pint fish stock stirring all the time and boil for 2 or 3 minutes. Add sauce to fish and rice and season well.

Rinse mould with cold water and decorate the bottom with tomato slices. Make some aspic jelly, following the instructions on the packet, and pour ¼ pint over the tomato slices. Leave to set before filling with fish and rice mixture. When set, turn out and decorate with sliced cucumber and watercress.

42. Fish Mousse

12 oz. flaked cooked fish
½ oz. (1 dsp.) gelatine
¼ pint white wine
½ diced green pepper

1 teacup diced cucumber
¼ pint double cream
sea salt, pepper

Soak gelatine in white wine and dissolve over low heat. Stir into fish. Blanch the diced pepper. Add cucumber, green pepper, salt and pepper to the fish and lastly add the half-whipped cream. Turn into a lightly oiled cake tin and leave to set. Turn out and garnish with watercress and cucumber. Serve with mayonnaise if liked.

43. Fish Slaw

1 lb. cod fillet	2 oz. raisins
½ lb. dutch cabbage	sea salt, pepper, garlic powder
½ lb. carrots	½ pint mayonnaise (see page
1 apple	11)
1 orange	

Simmer fish in boiling salted water for ½ hour. Cool and bone the fish. Shred cabbage and carrots, peel orange and apple and cut into small pieces. Mix fruit, fish, vegetables and raisins together in large bowl. Season well and stir in mayonnaise.

44. Fish and Rice Salad

1 lb. white fish or salmon	2 shallots
½ lb. cooked natural rice	2 oz. chopped parsley
½ lb. chopped raw mushrooms	2 oz. salad cream or mayon-
sea salt, pepper, garlic powder	naise (see page 11)
3 hard-boiled eggs	

Cook fish in boiling salted water, cool and bone. Flake the fish into a bowl and add to it the cooked rice, chopped raw mushrooms, the finely chopped hard-boiled eggs, parsley, chopped shallots, sea salt, pepper and garlic powder. Mix well and stir in mayonnaise.

45. Fish Mayonnaise

1½ lb. cooked white fish or salmon	*Mayonnaise*
	2 egg yolks
2 hard-boiled eggs	sea salt and pepper
½ sliced cucumber	½ pint olive oil
	1 dsp. apple cider vinegar

Beat the raw egg yolks in a cold basin or liquidizer; add sea salt and pepper, then the vinegar. Beat well. Add the olive oil slowly beating all the time until the mixture is thick and creamy.

33

Place the fish in egg-size lumps on serving dish, cover with mayonnaise and garnish with slices of hard-boiled eggs and cucumber.

46. Lobster Creams

½ lb. cooked lobster	sea salt and pepper
½ oz. gelatine	1 teasp. lemon juice
4 tbs. aspic jelly	¼ pint evaporated milk
4 tbs. white sauce	parsley to garnish

Chop and pound the lobster. Dissolve the gelatine in the aspic jelly. Mix the lobster with the white sauce, seasonings and lemon juice. Mix in the aspic jelly and stir well. Whip the evaporated milk and fold into the mixture. When just setting pour into individual dishes and garnish with parsley.

47. Lobster Soufflé

1 good-sized cooked lobster	1½ oz. butter
1 pint water	1 tbs. chopped chives
4 oz. dry white wine	½ oz. gelatine
1 onion	¼ pint double cream
1 oz. fennel	3 egg whites
1½ oz. plain wholewheat flour	

Remove the flesh from the lobster and place it in a bowl. Crush the shell and let it simmer in the water and white wine for 1 hour together with the onion and a little fennel. Strain off and keep the stock. Melt the butter in a saucepan, stir in the flour and gradually add ¾ pint stock; when thick add the flaked lobster flesh and chopped chives and simmer for a few more minutes. Dissolve the gelatine in a little hot water or stock and add to mixture; do not boil. Let it cool then stir in the double cream. When the mixture has almost set fold in the stiffly beaten egg whites, chill and re-set in refrigerator.

48. Salmon Relish

½ lb. cooked salmon	¾ oz. gelatine
1 lb. cooked peas	½ pint hot water
1 cucumber	4 oz. apple cider vinegar
3 tomatoes	2 tbs. mayonnaise (see page
1 lettuce	11)

Dissolve gelatine in hot water and add the vinegar. When cool pour a little into a mould and leave to set. Sprinkle some peas round the sides and at the bottom. Mix 1 tbs. of liquid gelatine mixture with mayonnaise and pour into bottom of mould. Mash the salmon, stir in the rest of the peas and the gelatine mixture. Pour into mould when nearly set. Spread lettuce leaves on serving dish then turn out the mould on to the leaves and decorate dish with cucumber and tomato slices.

49. Salmon Mousse

8 oz. cooked salmon	½ pint milk
3 tbs. double cream	1 oz. butter
1 dsp. tomato purée	1 oz. plain wholewheat flour
1 teasp. lemon juice	sea salt and pepper
¼ oz. gelatine	1 tbs. chopped parsley

Make white sauce with butter, flour and milk, season well and leave to cool. Flake salmon and mix with cream, tomato purée and lemon juice. Add the white sauce and adjust seasoning. Dissolve gelatine in hot water, cool and stir into mixture. Add chopped parsley. Pour into individual dishes and refrigerate.

50. Prawn Salad

1 pint cooked shelled prawns

Marinade
4 tbs. corn oil
2 tbs. lemon juice
sea salt and pepper
½ clove chopped garlic

Dressing
3 tbs. corn oil
1 tbs. apple cider vinegar
sea salt, pepper, brown sugar
(1 pinch)
(shake ingredients well together)

1 lettuce   6 stuffed olives   1 bundle watercress

Pour marinade over prawns and leave for 2 hours. Remove prawns and place on a bed of lettuce leaves, cover with dressing and decorate with watercress and stuffed olives.

51. Shrimp Mousse

1 carton of potted shrimps
1 tbs. tomato purée
1 lb. sieved cottage cheese
1 teasp. gelatine

sea salt and pepper
1 bundle watercress
slices of cucumber

Gently heat the potted shrimps in a heavy saucepan, stir in the tomato purée and combine the mixture with the cottage cheese. Dissolve the gelatine in 2 tbs. of water and stir into mixture. Season well and turn into an oiled mould. Garnish with watercress and cucumber.

52. Soused Herrings

8 herrings
3 tbs. plain wholewheat flour
3 small bay leaves
1 blade of mace
2 cloves

6 black peppercorns
¾ pint apple cider vinegar
½ pint water
sea salt and pepper

Scale, wash, trim and fillet fish. Mix flour with salt and pepper. Dip herrings in mixture and shake off the surplus flour. Roll

36

up each fillet from head to tail. Pack rolls in fireproof dish. Cut bay leaves in half and place between the fish. Add spices. Mix vinegar and water together just to cover the herrings. Cook in slow oven 350 °F. (Reg. 3–4) for 1 hour.

53. Scrambled Fish

6 eggs	half a cup of mayonnaise (see
3 oz. smoked haddock	page 11)
(cooked)	sea salt, pepper
2 oz. butter	chopped parsley, chives
2 tbs. cream	

Melt the butter in a pan and pour in the beaten eggs seasoned with salt and pepper. When they are nearly cooked stir in the flaked fish and cream. Leave to cool then stir in the mayonnaise. Serve sprinkled with chopped chives and parsley.

54. Fish Pancakes

Batter	*Filling*
4 oz. wholewheat flour	8 oz. white fish (cooked)
sea salt and pepper	1 oz. butter
1 egg	1 oz. wholewheat flour
½ pint of milk	½ pint milk
butter for frying	sea salt and pepper
	2 tbs. cream

Make batter by beating flour, egg, milk, salt and pepper together for 10 minutes. Fry 4 thin pancakes in butter and put on one side. Make white sauce, using 1 oz. butter mixed with 1 oz. wholewheat flour, adding the warmed milk gradually, sea salt, pepper and finally the cream. Put half this sauce aside to pour over the pancakes and mix the rest with the cooked fish. Fill the pancakes, roll up and cover with white sauce.

55. Baked Fish Roll

Pastry
8 oz. wholewheat flour
3 oz. lard
3 oz. margarine
2 oz. water
sea salt
1 beaten egg, or milk

Filling
8 oz. tinned salmon or any white fish

3 tbs. grated cheese
1 tbs. chopped parsley
sprinkling of grated nutmeg

Sauce
2 oz. butter, 2 oz. wholewheat flour
$\frac{1}{2}$ pint hot milk, anchovy essence to taste

Rub the lard and margarine into the salted flour and mix to a dough with cold water. Put in a cool place. Make a thick white sauce by melting the butter in a pan, stirring in the flour, then gradually adding the hot milk and a few drops of anchovy essence. Mix the fish, cheese, parsley and nutmeg into this sauce and allow to cool. Roll out pastry, spread filling down the centre. Fold over pastry sealing well and paint with milk or beaten egg. Bake in oven 350 °F. (Reg. 4) for 30–40 minutes.

56. Fish and Bacon Pie

$1\frac{1}{2}$ lb. white fish
2 oz. wholewheat flour
2 oz. butter or margarine
1 pint milk

sea salt, pepper
4 oz. grated cheddar cheese
2 oz. chopped parsley
4 rashers streaky bacon

Cut fish into the required number of portions, place on greased tray and bake for 20 minutes in oven 350 °F. (Reg. 4). Melt butter or margarine in a saucepan, add the flour then the warmed milk, simmer until thick and creamy, stirring all the time. Season well then remove from heat and add the grated cheese and chopped parsley. Place the fish in the serving dish, grill the bacon rashers and place one rasher on top of each piece of fish and cover with cheese sauce.

57. Orange Plaice

4 fillets of plaice
2 oranges
1 lemon
4 oz. mayonnaise (see page 11)
2 oz. butter
paprika
sea salt and pepper
8 anchovy fillets
2 oz. black olives
1 bunch watercress

Skin the fish, sprinkle with seasonings, lemon juice, orange juice and the rind of 1 orange. Roll them up tightly. Lay the fish in a well-buttered casserole, dot with butter and the juice of 1 orange; cover and cook in oven 350 °F. (Reg. 4) for 20 minutes. When cooked transfer fish to serving dish, sprinkle with orange juice again and cover with hot mayonnaise. Sprinkle with paprika and decorate with anchovy fillets, watercress and black olives.

58. French Fillets of Sole

3 fillets of sole
½ bottle of white wine
1 pint water
sea salt
2 oz. chopped onion
1 bouquet garni
2 oz. butter
2 oz. wholewheat flour
8 oz. white grapes, halved and stoned

Fillet the soles. Boil up the trimmings in a pint of salted water with the chopped onions. Put the fillets in a greased oven dish and cover with equal parts of strained stock and white wine; add the bouquet garni and cover with buttered paper. Bake in oven 350 °F. (Reg. 4) for 15 minutes. Make a roux with butter and flour and add the liquid from the oven dish. Add the rest of the wine and the halved grapes; when thick and creamy pour over fillets and serve.

59. Sole with Wine and Mushrooms

2 dover sole
½ pint water
½ pint white wine
1 bouquet garni
3 chopped shallots
4 oz. mushrooms
¼ teasp. fennel seeds

6 peppercorns
sea salt and pepper
½ pint double cream
2 egg yolks
2 oz. butter
juice of 1 lemon

Fillet two dover sole. Boil up bones and trimmings with bouquet garni, ½ pint water, ½ pint white wine, three chopped shallots and two sliced mushrooms. Add salt and pepper, peppercorns and fennel seeds and simmer for 15 minutes. Poach fillets gently in fish stock and wine for 7 minutes, then keep warm in low oven. Bring double cream to the boil and gradually add the strained fish stock, stirring all the time. Remove saucepan from the heat and add the two egg yolks which have first been mixed with a little of the hot sauce. Whisk well and return to the heat; simmer gently, but do not boil, until the sauce is thick and creamy. Place fillets in serving dish and pour sauce over them.

Remove stalks from remaining mushrooms, simmer the caps in butter and lemon juice and use them to garnish the dish.

60. Salmon Trout

1 good-sized salmon trout
1 cup of milk
½ lb. butter
juice of a lemon

4 oz. wholewheat flour
1 dsp. parsley (chopped)
sea salt and pepper

Clean and scale the trout. Dip in milk, then roll in seasoned flour. Sauté in butter until well browned on both sides. Sprinkle with lemon juice, pour over the juices from the pan and sprinkle with parsley.

61. Chinese Cod Steaks

2 lb. cod steaks	10 spring onions
4 oz. soya sauce	sea salt and pepper
¾ pint corn oil	2 oz. melted butter

Soak the steaks in soya sauce overnight. Clean and chop the spring onions using the green tops as well as the bulbs. Fry onions gently in the corn oil then add the steaks and fry gently on both sides. Place on serving dish, sprinkle with salt and pepper and pour over a little melted butter.

62. Chinese Scampi

1 lb. cooked scampi	2 dsp. cornflour
1 lb. egg noodles	3 dsp. soya sauce
2 chopped onions	½ cup water
½ lb. sliced mushrooms	½ cup chicken stock or bouil-
2 chopped green peppers	lon
4 tbs. vegetable oil	sea salt and pepper

Boil egg noodles in boiling salted water. Gently fry onions, peppers and mushrooms in vegetable oil for 5 minutes. Mix together the cornflour, soya sauce and water and add to the frying vegetables with ½ cup of chicken stock. Cover and cook gently until sauce thickens, stirring occasionally. Cut scampi in half and add to the sauce. Cook for a further 2 minutes then remove from heat and cover pan. Leave for 5 minutes then pour over the drained and seasoned noodles.

63. Fried Scampi with Tartare Sauce

1 lb. fresh or frozen scampi	*Sauce*
6 oz. wholewheat bread-	2 dsp. apple cider vinegar
crumbs	4 egg yolks
a little milk	4 tbs. olive oil
2 beaten eggs	1 teasp. each of chopped
vegetable oil for frying	parsley, capers and gher-
lemon slices	kins
parsley	sea salt, pepper and mustard

Dip shelled scampi in milk then in breadcrumbs. Dip in beaten egg and then in breadcrumbs again. Fry a few at a time in deep vegetable oil, drain on greaseproof paper and garnish with lemon slices and parsley.

Mix salt, pepper and mustard with vinegar in small bowl. Add egg yolks and beat well with wooden spoon. Gradually add oil, beating until thick and smooth. Add parsley, capers and gherkins.

Scampi may also be cooked in a batter made by beating 4 oz. salted wholewheat flour with 3 eggs and $\frac{1}{4}$ pint tepid water to which has been added a few drops of olive oil.

64. Baked Stuffed Haddock

4 thick fresh haddock steaks	1 cup wholewheat bread-
lemon juice	crumbs
1 chopped onion	pinch of tarragon, dill, sea salt
1 stick of chopped celery	and pepper
4 oz. sliced mushrooms	4 sliced tomatoes
$\frac{1}{2}$ pint milk	2 oz. butter

Place steaks in greased oven dish, sprinkle with lemon juice. Gently simmer onion, celery and mushrooms in milk for 5 minutes; add breadcrumbs, herbs and seasonings and pour over steaks. Top with sliced tomatoes, dot with butter and bake for 40 minutes in oven 375 °F. (Reg. 5).

65. Kedgeree

1 lb. smoked haddock	4 oz. chopped parsley
1 lb. natural brown rice	sea salt and pepper
2 hard-boiled eggs	4 oz. melted butter
$\frac{1}{2}$ pint milk	

Cook rice in boiling salted water for 20–30 minutes. Strain into colander and place under running cold water to separate the grains. Poach haddock gently in a little milk for 10 minutes. Drain and flake. Mix haddock with rice, add chopped hard-boiled eggs and parsley, pour over the melted butter and place in covered dish in moderate oven to heat through.

66. Haddock Omelette

8 oz. cooked smoked haddock	8 eggs (separated)
4 oz. butter	4 oz. grated cheddar cheese
½ pint double cream	sea salt and pepper

Heat 2 oz. butter with 4 tbs. cream in a pan and add the flaked fish. Let it cool. Beat the egg yolks, season with sea salt and pepper, add half the grated cheese and mix with the fish and cream. Whip up the egg whites and fold into the mixture. Make the omelette pan very hot, add 2 oz. butter and then the omelette mixture. Move the mixture around and when the base is set place it on a heatproof dish. Sprinkle with cheese and the remaining cream and brown under the grill.

67. Crab Pie

1 lb. crab meat	1 glass of dry sherry
2 oz. wholewheat bread-crumbs	1 tbs. chopped parsley
	sea salt and pepper
2 oz. tomato sauce	2 oz. butter
juice of ½ lemon	

Mix all ingredients together, except the butter, and simmer gently for 15 minutes. Add 2 oz. butter cut into small pieces and when the butter is well mixed in put the mixture into a shallow pie-dish and brown under the grill.

68. Crab Stew

1 lb. crab meat (cooked)	½ teasp. Worcester sauce
½ pint double cream	sea salt, pepper and mustard
1 lemon	1 glass dry sherry
2 stalks of chopped celery	

Simmer the double cream with the grated rind and juice of the lemon and the chopped celery for 10 minutes. Add the Worcester sauce, sea salt, pepper and a pinch of mustard, then the crab meat and sherry. Serve with boiled rice.

69. Prawn Risotto

6 oz. brown rice	2 onions
8 oz. cooked prawns	2 oz. parmesan cheese
2 tomatoes	1 pint stock (more if
1 green pepper	necessary)
3 oz. butter	

Chop onions and de-seeded green pepper and fry gently in butter until soft. Stir in the rice and cook until translucent. Add stock and simmer gently until all the liquid is absorbed and the rice is soft. Stir in two tomatoes, skinned and sliced, and then the prawns. Heat through and just before serving stir in the parmesan cheese. Serve with more cheese.

70. Prawn Curry

8 oz. cooked prawns	juice of $\frac{1}{2}$ a lemon
3 oz. butter	pinch of sea salt
1 chopped onion	1 clove of garlic
4 oz. curry powder	6 skinned tomatoes sliced
$\frac{1}{2}$ oz. wholewheat flour	2 oz. cream
1 teasp. turmeric powder	boiled natural brown rice to
1 teasp. powdered ginger	serve
$\frac{1}{2}$ pint stock	

Melt the butter in a heavy saucepan, add the chopped onion and cook until tender. Add the curry powder, flour, turmeric and ginger. Cook for 1 minute. Stir in the stock, lemon juice, salt, garlic and skinned sliced tomatoes. Bring to the boil. Cover and simmer gently for 20 minutes. Add the prawns and cook for a further 5 minutes. Remove from the heat and add the cream. Serve with plenty of natural brown rice.

71. Creamed Prawns

8 oz. cooked prawns	4 oz. chopped parsley
4 oz. sliced mushrooms	sea salt and pepper
2 oz. butter	$\frac{1}{4}$ pint milk
2 oz. wholewheat flour	$\frac{1}{4}$ pint single cream
3 teasp. sherry	

Cook sliced mushrooms gently in the butter, stir in the whole-wheat flour, sea salt and pepper. Pour in the milk and cream, stirring all the time until thick and creamy. Add $\frac{1}{2}$ lb. cooked prawns and then the sherry. Sprinkle with parsley and serve.

72. Cheese Prawns

8 oz. cooked prawns	$\frac{1}{2}$ pint milk
2 oz. butter	2 oz. grated cheese
2 oz. wholewheat flour	sea salt and pepper

Melt the butter in a saucepan and add the flour, stir for a minute or two then gradually add the milk; bring to the boil and allow to thicken. Remove from heat and stir in the grated cheese, sea salt and pepper. Add the prawns, turn into an ovenproof dish, sprinkle with cheese and put under the grill for a few minutes.

73. Lobster Newburg

$1\frac{1}{2}$ lb. lobster	pinch of paprika
$\frac{1}{4}$ pint white wine	$\frac{1}{4}$ pint double cream
$\frac{1}{2}$ lb. mushrooms	sea salt and pepper
2 oz. butter	10 oz. natural brown rice
2 egg yolks	

Cook the rice in boiling salted water, strain it, run cold water through it, and place in warm oven to dry out. Remove the flesh from the lobster. Cut the meat into small pieces and cook in butter over a low heat. Pour in the white wine and let it cook for 15 minutes; add 3 tbs. cream, the finely sliced mushrooms, paprika, sea salt and pepper and simmer for a further 15 minutes. Mix the egg yolks with 2 tbs. cream, add sea salt and pepper and add this to the fish very gradually; stir gently until the sauce is creamy but do not let it boil. Arrange the lobster and the sauce on a bed of rice and decorate with the small claws.

74. Lobster Croquettes

8 oz. cooked lobster or crab meat
3 oz. sliced mushrooms
2 oz. butter
½ oz. grated onion
¼ pint single cream
1 egg yolk
sea salt and pepper
paprika
4 oz. seasoned wholewheat flour
4 oz. wholewheat bread-crumbs
2 beaten eggs for coating
vegetable oil for frying

Cook the grated onion and the sliced mushrooms in the butter, then add the lobster meat and cook with the lid on for 5 minutes very gently. Remove from heat, season well, and add the egg yolk beaten into the cream. Let the mixture cool then shape into balls, coat with seasoned flour, beaten egg and breadcrumbs. Fry in deep vegetable oil.

75. Stuffed Herrings

4 herrings
½ lb. chopped apples
1 dsp. grated onion
1 teasp. barbados sugar
2 oz. fresh wholewheat bread-crumbs
½ oz. melted butter
sea salt and pepper
2 oz. chopped parsley

Scale, wash and trim fish. Split open flat and remove the backbone and small bones. Season with sea salt and pepper. Mix apple, onion, parsley and sugar with 1½ oz. wholewheat breadcrumbs; season well. Spread this stuffing over the herrings and roll them up from head to tail. Place in a greased fireproof dish, sprinkle with rest of breadcrumbs and pour over melted butter. Bake in moderate oven 375 °F. (Reg. 5) for 30–35 minutes.

76. Scallops

8–12 scallops
¼ pint white wine
¼ pint water
1 bouquet garni
2 oz. butter
1 shallot
¼ lb. sliced mushrooms

1 oz. wholewheat flour
¼ pint milk
1 tbs. wholewheat bread-
   crumbs
a little melted butter
sea salt

Boil the scallops gently for about 10 minutes or until tender in ¼ pint water and ¼ pint white wine with 1 bouquet garni and some sea salt. Remove scallops, reserving the liquid, and cut into small pieces. Melt the butter in a saucepan, add the shallot and the sliced mushrooms and cook gently for 5 minutes. Add the flour and the strained liquid from the scallops. Stir until boiling, simmer for a few minutes then add the milk gradually and reduce to a creamy consistency. Add the scallops and pour into shells. Sprinkle with wholewheat breadcrumbs and a little melted butter and brown under the grill.

4-Meat Dishes

Beef
77. Steak and Kidney
    Pudding
78. Braised Steak
79. Beef Goulash
80. Spiced Baked Beef
81. Beef Casserole
82. Italian Beef Casserole
83. Beef Bourguignon
84. Beef Olives
85. Meat Pasties
86. Chile Con Carne
87. Turkish Mince
88. Savoury Meat Roll
89. Spiced Beef Loaf
90. Beef and Potato Pie

Veal
91. Stuffed Fillet of Veal
92. Veal and Ham Pie
93. Minced Veal Pie
94. Paprika Veal Fillets
95. Hungarian Goulash
96. Casserole of Veal
97. Blanquette of Veal
98. Veal Galantine
99. Curried Veal

100. Roast Veal with
     Oranges and Wine
101. Veal and Bacon Rolls

Pork and Ham
102. French Roast Pork
103. Sausage Rolls
104. Spiced Ham Bake
105. Country Pork Chops
106. Pork and Veal Pie
107. Stuffed Crown Roast
     of Pork
108. Malayan Pork with
     Cauliflower
109. Hungarian Pork Dish
110. Sweet and Sour Pork

Lamb
111. Curried Lamb
     Malayan Style
112. Stuffed Lamb
113. Paprika Lamb
114. Moussaka
115. Navarin of Mutton
     or Lamb
116. Noisettes of Lamb
     with Mushrooms

77. Steak and Kidney Pudding

1 lb. stewing steak	sea salt and pepper
½ lb. ox kidney	1 cup chicken stock
1 large onion	2 cups water
1 tbs. chopped parsley	1 lb. plain wholewheat flour
3 oz. sliced mushrooms	4 oz. beef suet

Chop meat into cubes and mix with the chopped parsley, sliced onion, and the sliced mushrooms. Put into bowl and cover with chicken stock and water. Season well and leave to marinate overnight.

Rub the suet into the seasoned flour and mix to a fairly stiff dough with a little cold water. Roll out and line a 2 lb. pudding basin. Put the meat mixture into the lined basin and cover with layer of suet pastry. Seal well by pressing down, then trim the edges. Cover basin with white cloth and tie it up, leaving a loop to lift it out with. Cook slowly in a saucepan of water with a lid on. It should take about 5½ to 6 hours.

78. Braised Steak

1½ lb. stewing steak	1 bouquet garni
2 oz. butter	sea salt and pepper
½ lb. carrots	3 oz. wholewheat flour
½ lb. onions	1 teasp. Marmite
1½ pints stock	1 dsp. chopped parsley

Slice meat into four good thick steaks. Fry gently in butter on each side for a few minutes then place in casserole. Slice and fry carrots and onions and add to casserole. Pour in stock, season well, add bouquet garni. Cover casserole and cook in oven 375 °F. (Reg. 5) for 2 hours or until meat is tender. Remove bouquet garni, thicken stock with 3 oz. wholewheat flour, add Marmite and parsley and replace in oven for a further 15 minutes.

79. Beef Goulash

1½ lb. stewing steak	1 teasp. caraway seeds
½ lb. onions	1 chopped clove garlic
3 oz. dripping	1 lb. potatoes
1½ pints stock	1 teasp. paprika powder
2 green peppers	sea salt and pepper
½ lb. tomatoes	1 small carton yoghourt

Chop meat into cubes and slice the onions. Fry the onions in the dripping, add the meat and cook for about 5 minutes, stirring all the time. Add stock, cover and cook for ½ hour gently. Chop the tomatoes and peppers removing pith and seeds, add to meat together with the caraway seeds and garlic. Simmer for a further ½ hour. Add diced potatoes and paprika powder and salt and pepper to taste. Add more stock or water to cover the potatoes and simmer for a further ¾ hour. Just before serving stir in the yoghourt.

80. Spiced Baked Beef

4 lb. topside beef	½ oz. saltpetre
1 clove garlic	1 bay leaf
2 oz. barbados sugar	6 oz. sea salt
½ oz. allspice	

Chop garlic very finely; mix with sugar and rub this mixture into and all over the meat. Leave overnight. Next day rub in the other ingredients having first chopped the bay leaf as finely as possible. Keep the spiced meat in a deep dish for several days. At the end of this time, wash the meat and wrap it in foil to make an airtight parcel. Put the parcel in a baking tin with a few tablespoons of water and bake in oven 350 °F. (Reg. 4) for 1½–2 hours. Allow to cool before removing the foil and serve with creamy horseradish sauce.

81. Beef Casserole

1½ lb. stewing steak
4 tbs. butter
2 tbs. olive oil
1 lb. tomatoes, skinned and de-seeded
boiled potatoes, peeled and sliced

2 tbs. tomato paste
2 sprigs of thyme
2 bay leaves
sea salt and pepper
2 cloves of garlic
water, stock or dry white wine

Cut beef into cubes and sauté in butter and olive oil until well browned. Add chopped tomatoes, tomato paste, thyme, bay leaves, sea salt and pepper to taste. Add unpeeled smashed cloves of garlic and put the mixture in an ovenproof casserole. Cover with stock, water or dry white wine. Cook for 3 hours in oven 375 °F. (Reg. 5). Just before serving add some sliced cooked potatoes.

82. Italian Beef Casserole

2 lb. skirt of beef
½ calf's foot
½ lb. green bacon
1 oz. butter
3 tbs. olive oil
4 oz. mushrooms
1 bouquet garni

1 large onion
1 clove garlic
2 tbs. tomato purée
½ bottle red wine
sea salt and pepper
2 oz. green olives
1 tbs. chopped parsley

Cut the calf's foot and bacon into small pieces and put in a pan of cold water and bring to the boil. Remove from water, drain and dry thoroughly. Cut the beef into cubes and fry in olive oil and butter, together with the calf's foot and bacon until golden brown. Put in a casserole, add the sliced onions, mushrooms and garlic and the rest of the ingredients except the olives and the parsley. Cover tightly and cook in oven 350 °F. (Reg. 4) for 3½ hours. Add the olives ½ hour before the end of the cooking time. Remove the bouquet garni and sprinkle the casserole with chopped parsley.

83. Beef Bourguignon

$1\frac{1}{2}$ lb. chuck steak
4 oz. wholewheat flour
4 tbs. olive oil
4 tbs. butter
$\frac{1}{4}$ lb. salt pork, diced
2 carrots
1 leek
4 shallots
1 onion
1 clove of garlic
1 bouquet garni
$\frac{1}{2}$ bottle burgundy

beef stock or water
$\frac{1}{2}$ calf's foot

For later addition
1 tbs. wholewheat flour
1 tbs. butter
18 button onions
2 oz. barbados sugar
12 button mushrooms
lemon juice
chopped parsley
sea salt, pepper

Cut beef into cubes and roll in flour. Sauté salt pork in half the oil and butter until crisp and brown. Transfer pork to large ovenproof casserole. Brown beef well in remaining fat, season well and add to casserole. Chop the vegetables, sauté in frying pan until brown and transfer to casserole. Add the calf's foot and bouquet garni. Pour in most of the wine and enough water or stock to cover the meat and vegetables. Cover and cook in oven 350 °F. (Reg. 4) for 2 hours. Remove fat from the sauce and stir in 1 tbs. butter worked with 1 tbs. wholewheat flour; cover and continue to cook gently in oven for a further $2\frac{1}{2}$ hours.

Brown the small onions in a saucepan with a little butter and sugar. Add remaining red wine, cover and cook over low flame until the onions are almost tender. Keep warm. Sauté mushrooms in remaining butter and oil and a little lemon juice. When the meat is tender remove calf's foot and bouquet garni, correct seasoning, add onions and mushrooms and sprinkle well with chopped parsley.

84. Beef Olives

1 lb. rump steak	1 oz. suet
1 carrot	½ egg
1 turnip	2 oz. wholewheat bread-
1 onion	crumbs
1 oz. butter	1 tbs. chopped parsley
1 oz. wholewheat flour	sea salt and pepper
¾ pint stock	

Cut all the vegetables into small pieces and fry in butter. Add flour and allow to brown. Add stock. Cut the steak into oblong pieces. Mix the suet, parsley, breadcrumbs and seasoning with the egg. Spread on steak and roll up. Tie with thread and place in pan. Simmer gently for 2½–3 hours. Remove thread and pour gravy and vegetables round beef olives.

85. Meat Pasties

6 oz. wholewheat flour	*Filling*
3 oz. lard	6 oz. chuck steak (thinly
3 oz. margarine	sliced)
sea salt and pepper	1 small diced potato
a little cold water	1 small chopped onion
	seasoned wholewheat flour

Mix flour and salt together, rub in the lard and then add the water to make a soft lump. Roll out on well-floured board and spread with dots of margarine. Bring each corner into the middle and roll out into a rectangle. Fold in three and roll out again. Leave to rest for 20 minutes and roll out and fold again. Repeat twice more. Cut the pastry into four circles about 6 inches across. Lay on your filling mixed with seasoned flour, damp the pastry edges and fold over very firmly. Bake in oven 375 °F. (Reg. 5) for 25 minutes.

86. Chile Con Carne

1½ lb. minced beef
3 oz. olive oil
1 clove of garlic
½ lb. skinned and sliced toma-
    toes
¼ lb. sliced onions

1 pint water or stock
1 dsp. cumin seed
2 lb. red kidney beans
2 chopped chilli peppers
sea salt and pepper

Fry the meat in a heavy saucepan with a little olive oil. When it is brown add the chopped garlic, sliced tomatoes, chopped onions and the salt and pepper. Add the cumin seed, stock and the kidney beans soaked overnight. Bring to the boil and simmer for 2 hours. Add the chilli peppers or powder as desired and simmer for a further 20 minutes before serving with natural brown rice.

87. Turkish Mince

2 lb. minced beef
5 dsp. olive oil
4 peeled sliced tomatoes
1 grated onion
1 chopped green pepper
1 teasp. grated nutmeg
6 crushed peppercorns
½ clove garlic crushed
1 teasp. fennel

1 teasp. thyme
1 crushed bay leaf
2 tbs. tomato paste
½ glass red wine
1 chicken bouillon cube
1 cup stock
4 tbs. wholewheat flour
8 oz. grated cheddar cheese
sea salt and pepper

Gently heat the oil in a large heavy saucepan. Add tomatoes, onion, green pepper and cook gently for about 10 minutes. Add herbs, nutmeg, garlic, peppercorns and tomato paste. Stir well, adding the red wine. Add meat then stir in the flour mixed to a smooth paste with a little cold water or stock. Add 1 cup of stock and the crushed bouillon cube. Simmer for 5 minutes, stirring constantly and adding seasoning and a little more liquid if necessary. Transfer to earthenware dish and sprinkle over the grated cheese.

88. Savoury Meat Roll

$1\frac{1}{2}$ lb. minced beef
$\frac{1}{4}$ lb. onions
$\frac{1}{2}$ lb. carrots
2 oz. chopped parsley
1 oz. curry powder
4 oz. wholewheat flour
a little stock or water
sea salt and pepper

1 beaten egg

Pastry
1 lb. wholewheat flour
6 oz. lard
6 oz. margarine
sea salt and pepper
4 oz. (approx.) cold water

Rub lard and margarine into seasoned flour and mix to a workable dough with cold water. Roll out into rectangular shape on well-floured board.

Cook minced beef with minced carrots and onions for about $1\frac{1}{2}$ hours. Drain off all liquid and thicken mince with wholewheat flour rubbed to a smooth paste with a little water or stock. Add chopped parsley and curry powder and salt and pepper and cook for 10 minutes more. Leave to cool and thicken. Place on pastry, roll up firmly, paint with beaten egg, score the top, and bake in oven 375 °F. (Reg. 5) for $\frac{3}{4}$ hour.

89. Spiced Beef Loaf

2 lb. minced beef
6 rashers streaky bacon
$\frac{1}{2}$ teasp. each of allspice, black
  pepper, sea salt, thyme and
  basil

4 tbs. red wine or port
1 clove garlic

Put the minced beef in a bowl and add to it all the seasonings and herbs together with the finely chopped clove of garlic. Remove the rind from the bacon, cut it in small dice and add to the meat mixture. Lastly add the wine. Place the meat in the centre of a piece of buttered greaseproof paper forming it into a fat sausage. Twist the edges and the ends of the paper together, put the parcel into a baking tin and add 1 cup of cold water. Cook in moderate oven 350 °F. (Reg. 4) for 1 hour.

Leave until quite cold before unwrapping the meat loaf. Slice and eat with chutney, pickles and green salad.

90. Beef and Potato Pie

1 lb. minced beef	1 chopped onion
4 tbs. milk	1 teasp. sea salt
2 tbs. tomato sauce	½ teasp. dry mustard, thyme
2 oz. quick-cooking porridge	and pepper
oats	1½ lb. potatoes
1 egg	1 tbs. parmesan cheese

Combine all the ingredients except the potatoes and cheese, put in a baking tin and bake in oven 350 °F. (Reg. 4) for 30 minutes. Boil 1½ lb. potatoes. Mash them with milk and butter and season well. Add 1 tbs. grated parmesan cheese. Put the potato on top of the meat mixture. Brush the surface with melted butter, sprinkle with grated cheese and bake for a further 20 minutes.

91. Stuffed Fillet of Veal

4 thin slices of veal	2 onions
4 oz. minced ham	3 tomatoes
1 egg	¼ bottle of red wine
1 dsp. chopped parsley	sea salt and pepper
2 oz. butter	

Mix the minced ham with the chopped parsley, season well and stir in the beaten egg. Place one-quarter of this stuffing in the middle of each piece of veal, roll up tightly and secure with thread. Melt butter in heavy pan, add the fillets and brown all over. Add sliced onions, chopped and peeled tomatoes, 2 cupfuls of red wine, sea salt and pepper. Put a lid on the pan and simmer for 1½ hours. Put fillets on a warm dish and pour the gravy over them.

92. Veal and Ham Pie (Loaf)

Hot water crust
4 oz. lard
6 tbs. water
12 oz. plain wholewheat flour
½ teasp. sea salt
1 beaten egg

Filling
1 lb. fillet of veal

1 teasp. chopped parsley
1 teasp. grated lemon rind
4 oz. ham
2 hard-boiled eggs
¼ pint stock
sea salt and pepper
1 dsp. gelatine

Bring the lard and the water to the boil, add the salted whole-wheat flour, mix well and leave to cool (approx. 30 minutes).

Cut the veal into small cubes and mix with parsley, lemon rind, sea salt and pepper. Add the diced ham.

Take two-thirds of the pastry and roll out. Line a 9-inch loaf tin with pastry reserving the remainder for the lid and decorations. Fill the tin with the veal and ham mixture placing the hard-boiled eggs one each end in the middle of the meat mixture. Pour in a little stock to moisten. Brush the top edge of the pastry with water and press on the lid. Decorate the edge, make a hole in the centre and decorate with pastry rose and leaves. Brush the top with beaten egg and bake in oven 375 °F. (Reg. 5) for 1½ hours. After 1 hour remove pie from tin, brush sides with beaten egg and return to oven for remainder of cooking time. Cool on cake rack. Dissolve gelatine in a little hot stock, pour through hole and leave pie to set.

93. Minced Veal Pie

¾ lb. minced veal (cooked)
¼ lb. minced ham (cooked)
1 teasp. grated lemon rind
1 teasp. chopped parsley
sea salt and pepper
1 tbs. grated cheddar cheese
1 tbs. wholewheat bread-crumbs

Sauce
1½ oz. butter
1½ oz. plain wholewheat flour
¾ pint mixed veal stock and milk
½ teasp. mixed mustard, sea salt and pepper

58

Make a white sauce with the butter, flour and liquid, add the seasoning and the mustard. Put it in a double saucepan with the veal, ham, lemon rind, parsley and seasoning and heat together thoroughly. Turn the mixture into a fireproof dish, sprinkle with breadcrumbs and grated cheese and grill lightly to brown.

94. Paprika Veal Fillets

½ lb. fillet of veal, cut very thinly
4 oz. butter
4 oz. onions
1 oz. red paprika powder
1 teasp. caraway seeds
½ pint veal stock
sea salt and pepper
3 green peppers
½ lb. tomatoes
small carton sour cream

Beat the fillets until very thin; sprinkle with sea salt and pepper. Heat butter and fry fillets 1 minute on each side. Remove from pan. Chop the onions and fry in the same fat; sprinkle in the paprika powder and mix well. Return meat to pan, add the caraway seeds and stock to reach the top of the meat. Slice the tomatoes and the peppers; cover the meat with these. Put on tight-fitting lid and simmer gently for 45 minutes until tender. Just before serving pour over the sour cream.

95. Hungarian Goulash

1 lb. stewing veal cut into cubes
1 oz. butter
½ lb. onions thinly sliced
1 clove of garlic
1 tbs. tomato paste
pinch of caraway seeds
1 tbs. paprika
1 tbs. wholewheat flour
sea salt and pepper
¾ pint stock
1 green pepper sliced and de-seeded
½ pint yoghourt

Brown the meat in the hot butter, then remove and fry the onions and crushed garlic. Add the flour, paprika, stock, seasoning, tomato paste, green pepper and caraway seeds and bring to simmering point. Add veal. Simmer gently for 1½

59

hours. Just before serving stir in the yoghourt, reheat and serve with rice or noodles.

96. Casserole of Veal

1½ lb. neck or breast of veal	½ pint stock
2 oz. streaky bacon	2 tbs. tomato paste
½ lb. onions	½ teasp. grated lemon rind
¼ lb. young carrots	1 dsp. chopped parsley

Divide meat into four nice chunky pieces. Cut up the streaky bacon and fry gently; place in casserole. Fry veal in bacon fat for 2 minutes on each side and remove to casserole. Slice the onions and the carrots and fry gently in the same fat; add to casserole. Stir stock into fat, add lemon rind, parsley and tomato paste and cook gently for a few minutes. Pour into casserole, cover with tight lid and cook in oven 350 °F. (Reg. 4) for 1½ hours.

97. Blanquette of Veal

1½ lb. cubed stewing veal	1 teasp. chopped parsley
2 tbs. butter	4 oz. mushrooms
1 tbs. wholewheat flour	1 sliced carrot
sea salt and pepper	2 sliced onions
1 pint stock or water	1 clove garlic
1 bay leaf	1 egg
pinch of thyme	1 lemon

Soak veal in cold water for 15 minutes; dry well. Melt the butter in a heavy pan and fry veal gently. Sprinkle with wholewheat flour and enough stock to cover. Add the sea salt, pepper, thyme, parsley, bay leaf, sliced mushrooms, carrot, onions and garlic. Cover and simmer for 2 hours. Just before serving beat up an egg with the juice of a lemon. Add to this some of the hot but not boiling stock, gradually stirring it into the egg. Mix this thickened gravy in with the rest of the stock and the meat. Serve with natural brown rice.

98. Veal Galantine

½ lb. lean veal	sea salt and pepper
½ lb. cooked ham	grated rind of 1 lemon
½ lb. fat bacon	4 oz. fresh wholewheat bread-
1 small onion	crumbs
1 beaten egg	1 tbs. chopped parsley
1 clove garlic	stock or water to cover

Mince finely together the veal, ham, bacon, onion and garlic. Add seasoning, lemon rind, breadcrumbs and parsley. Mix in the beaten egg and form into loaf shape. Place in centre of clean cloth, roll up and tie firmly at both ends. Simmer in stock to cover for 2 hours. Cool slightly and tighten the cloth. Put a weight on top and leave overnight. Slice as required.

99. Curried Veal

1½ lb. fillet of veal (cubed)	bouquet garni
8 oz. butter	1 cooking apple
1 large chopped onion	2 egg yolks
2 diced carrots	juice of ½ lemon
1½ dsp. curry powder	2 slices diced pineapple
1 tbs. wholewheat flour	sea salt and pepper
1 oz. desiccated coconut	1 oz. grilled flaked almonds
½ gill boiling water	natural brown rice
½ pint stock	

Curry sauce: Fry the onion in 2 oz. butter, add the carrots and sauté lightly. Stir in curry powder and flour. Cook for a few minutes, then stir in the stock, the coconut and boiling water. Add bouquet garni and bring to the boil; add apple and cook gently for ½ hour. Sieve sauce and keep warm in double boiler.

Hollandaise sauce: Put the two egg yolks and the lemon juice in a basin over a saucepan of boiling water; stir continuously whilst adding 4 oz. butter a little at a time. Do not overheat or the sauce will curdle.

Sauté the veal in 2 oz. butter for a few minutes, add the diced pineapple and curry sauce and leave on gentle heat for 10 minutes. Add hollandaise sauce very slowly, season well, and put into serving dish; cover with flaked almonds and serve with natural brown rice.

100. Roast Veal with Oranges and Wine

2 lb. roasting veal (for roasting times see page 10)
2 lb. carrots
1 lb. onions
6 oranges
1 thick rasher of fat bacon
2 tbs. brandy
2 wineglasses dry white wine
sea salt and pepper
2 oz. butter
1 tbs. vegetable oil

Heat 2 oz. butter and 1 tbs. vegetable oil in a thick pan and brown the meat all over. Pour the brandy over the meat and set it alight. Add salt and pepper, the sliced carrots and onions and the dry white wine. Cover and cook gently for 1 hour. Add the juice of 4 oranges and simmer for a further 15 minutes. Place the roasted meat on a large serving dish, pour over it the juices from the pan and surround it with strips of crisply cooked fat bacon and the carrots and onions. Decorate with slices of orange.

101. Veal and Bacon Rolls

1 lb. fillet of veal cut in thin slices
juice and grated rind of 1 lemon
¼ lb. bacon rashers
2 oz. wholewheat flour
3 oz. butter
sea salt and pepper
1 large sliced onion
½ pint water
¼ pint red wine
1 bouquet garni
4 oz. sliced sautéed mushrooms

Sprinkle each slice of veal with lemon juice, salt and pepper. Place a rinded rasher of bacon on each piece and roll up and secure with thin string. Coat the rolls with wholewheat flour and fry gently in butter. Place the rolls of meat in a casserole and fry the sliced onion in the butter; cook until tender and pour into the casserole. Add the wine, water, lemon rind and bouquet garni. Cover with a lid and cook for 1 hour in oven 350 °F. (Reg. 4). Remove the string from the veal rolls and place on serving dish. Season sauce if necessary and pour over rolls. Garnish with sliced sautéed mushrooms.

102. French Roast Pork

1 boned hand of pork	4 oz. barbados sugar
1 teasp. sea salt	1 apple cut into segments
½ teasp. ground nutmeg	1 tbs. wholewheat flour
2 tbs. vegetable oil	butter
1 wineglass cider	

Rub the hand of pork all over with the teasp. sea salt and the nutmeg dissolved in 2 tbs. vegetable oil. Put in a hot oven 450 °F. (Reg. 8) for 10 minutes; then reduce to 350 °F. (Reg. 4) and add the cider and brown sugar. Roast for 2 hours basting frequently, and decorate with segments of apple dipped in flour and fried in butter.

103. Sausage Rolls

8 oz. wholewheat flour	3 oz. water
pinch of sea salt	½ lb. sausage meat
3 oz. margarine	1 dsp. chutney or pickle
3 oz. lard	1 beaten egg
1 dsp. lemon juice	

Cut margarine and lard into salted wholewheat flour, add the lemon juice then bind the ingredients into a soft dough with the water. Turn the dough on to the floured pastry board. Roll the pastry into a rectangle and cut the rectangle into three strips.

Mix the pickle or chutney with the sausage meat, season well and then divide into three equal pieces. Roll each of these

pieces into a sausage shape the same length as the pastry strips.
Lay one down the centre of each strip. Brush round the edges
of the pastry with beaten egg then roll it round the sausage
meat. Brush the outside of the roll with beaten egg, cut each
one into eight pieces and make an incision in each one. Bake
the sausage rolls in a hot oven 450 °F. (Reg. 8) for 10 minutes
then reduce the heat a little and cook for a further 15 minutes.

104. Spiced Ham Bake

3 lb. gammon
1½ lb. wholewheat flour
cold water

2 tbs. barbados sugar
cloves
small bottle ginger ale

Soak ham in cold water for about 2–3 hours, wipe dry and trim
off any discoloured parts. Make a flour and water paste and
wrap it round the ham, brushing joins with cold water before
pressing together to make a case. Put pastry-covered ham in
well-greased meat tin and bake in oven 375 °F. (Reg. 5) for
1½ hours. Remove ham from oven and whilst hot strip off
paste and remove outside rind. Rub ham fat with barbados
sugar then cut into a diamond pattern with a knife. Stud each
diamond with a clove. Place ham on rack in meat tin, sprinkle
with ginger ale and replace in hot oven 400 °F. (Reg. 6) for
15 minutes.

105. Country Pork Chops

4 thick pork chops
4 oz. sultanas
1 large cooking apple
rind of 1 orange

1 chopped cooked cabbage
sea salt and pepper
1 tbs. sherry
¼ pint stock

Brown the chops in hot fat in a frying pan over strong heat.
Mix sultanas, finely chopped apple and orange rind with the
cabbage; add pepper and salt to taste. Put the cabbage in a
heavy saucepan, lay the chops on top, cover with stock and
sherry. Cover saucepan and simmer gently for 1½ hours. Place

chops on serving dish, cover with cabbage and serve with creamed potatoes.

106. Pork and Veal Pie

Pastry
1 lb. wholewheat flour
6 oz. margarine
6 oz. lard
4 oz. water (approx.)
sea salt

Filling
12 oz. pork
12 oz. veal
a pinch of nutmeg and black
  pepper
1 wineglass white wine
1 egg yolk
2 eggs
sea salt
1 teacup cream

Cut the pork and veal into small pieces, dust them with pepper and nutmeg and pour over them the white wine. Leave to marinate overnight.

Rub the lard and margarine into the salted flour and mix to a soft dough with cold water. Roll out on a floured board and cut pieces to line the bottom and sides of a pie dish, reserving enough to make a lid. Drain the meat and place it in the pie dish. Fold in the edges of the pastry and cover with a pastry lid. Cut a hole in the centre of the lid. Brush with beaten egg yolk and bake in oven 400 °F. (Reg. 6) for 40 minutes.

Beat the two eggs with the cream; add salt to taste and pour into the pie through the hole in the top. Return to oven 350 °F. (Reg. 4) for a further ½ hour.

107. Stuffed Crown Roast of Pork

1 crown roast (prepared by the butcher): 2 ribs per person, cut through sufficiently to allow the joint to be rolled round to make a circle.

Stick small onions on the top of each chop and cook in slow oven 325 °F. (Reg. 3) for 35 minutes. Remove, fill centre with mashed potatoes and return to oven for a further ½ hour.

108. Malayan Pork with Cauliflower

1 cauliflower
6 oz. lean pork
4 crushed cloves of garlic
3 tbs. corn oil
1 tbs. soya sauce

1 tbs. cornflour
2 tbs. apple cider vinegar
pinch of chilli powder
sea salt and pepper

Break the cauliflower into small pieces, wash and drain them. Slice the pork finely. Fry the garlic in the oil then add the pork. Cook and stir for 1 minute. Add soya sauce and cauliflower. Mix well, add water to cover and add salt and pepper. Cook over low heat for 15 minutes. Mix the cornflour with a little cold water and add to mixture. When it thickens continue to cook it for 5 minutes. Add the apple cider vinegar and chilli powder and serve with natural brown rice.

109. Hungarian Pork Dish

1½ lb. pork fillet
2 rashers smoked streaky bacon
2 oz. lard
2 onions
1 teasp. paprika powder

¼ pint water or stock
1 green pepper
2 tomatoes
1 tbs. wholewheat flour
1 carton yoghourt or sour cream

Cut meat and bacon into strips and fry in hot lard. Add the finely chopped onions and the paprika powder. Stir until well blended. Add stock or water and cook for 5 minutes. Cover tightly and simmer for ½ hour adding more water if necessary; stir frequently. Add sliced green pepper and tomatoes and cook until meat is tender, approximately another ½ hour. Blend the sour cream with the flour and add when the pork is cooked, bring to the boil and serve at once.

110. Sweet and Sour Pork

2 lb. belly of pork (skinned and cubed)
2 oz. wholewheat flour
4 oz. soya sauce
2 oz. barbados sugar
5 oz. sweet vinegar pickles
1 pint stock
vegetable oil for frying

fried natural brown rice

Batter
4 oz. wholewheat flour
2 eggs
sea salt
4 oz. milk
2 oz. water

Make batter by beating eggs, milk and water in salted flour for 10 minutes.

Boil sugar, soya sauce and stock together. Add pickles. Thicken sauce by mixing flour with cold stock and adding to mixture. Boil for a further 5 minutes. Keep warm.

Dip pork cubes in batter and fry gently in vegetable oil for several minutes. Serve with plenty of fried natural rice and serve sauce either separately or stirred into pork cubes.

111. Curried Lamb Malayan Style

2½ lb. boned shoulder of lamb
3 oz. butter
6 oz. finely chopped onions
2½ tbs. curry powder
2 oz. finely chopped pre-served ginger
½ teasp. dried mint

1 teasp. barbados sugar
pinch black pepper
sea salt
4 oz. grated coconut
¼ pint water
juice of 2 lemons
¼ pint double cream

Side dishes
1 lb. natural brown rice cooked for 20 minutes in boiling salted water then mixed with 4 oz. currants, simmered in 1 wineglassful of red wine, and 1 chopped red pepper
8 oz. mango chutney
4 hard-boiled eggs sliced and dressed with a sauce made by boiling ¼ pint double cream with 1 tbs. sweet sherry and 1 dsp. curry powder

1 lb. sliced peeled tomatoes sprinkled with salt, sugar and oil
2 sliced shallots dressed with apple cider vinegar
2 sliced oranges
1 sliced cucumber dressed with oil and apple cider vinegar
1 bowl of oat crunchies
1 bowl desiccated coconut

Fry the onions in the butter then add the lamb cut into small pieces and brown well. Add the ginger, sugar, salt, pepper, curry powder and mint. Mix well, place lid on pan and cook gently for 15 minutes. Add the grated coconut and ¼ pint boiling water and continue to simmer with the lid on for 1 hour. Add the lemon juice, let this boil and then add the double cream and simmer for a further 15 minutes or until the lamb is really tender.

112. Stuffed Lamb

2 lb. best end neck of lamb	2 tbs. chopped parsley
1 beaten egg	¼ teasp. mixed chopped herbs
browned wholewheat bread-crumbs	grated rind and juice of ½ orange
2 oz. dripping	½ chopped onion
	1½ oz. butter
Stuffing	sea salt and pepper
8 tbs. wholewheat bread-crumbs	

To make the stuffing, mix together the breadcrumbs, parsley, herbs and orange rind. Cook the onions in the butter and add them to the stuffing; bind together with the orange juice and half the beaten egg. Season well.

Bone the meat and trim it with a sharp knife. Spread the stuffing over the meat and roll it up. Tie it firmly in several places with fine string. Brush over the top with beaten egg and cover with browned wholewheat breadcrumbs. Heat the dripping in a meat tin, put in the meat and baste well with dripping. Cook in oven 375 °F. (Reg. 5) for 1½ hours. Remove string and serve.

Meat Dishes

113. Paprika Lamb

2 lb. middle neck of lamb	1 tbs. chopped parsley
2 oz. butter	2 teasp. paprika
4 oz. minced onion	sea salt and pepper
1 lb. skinned and sliced toma-	¼ pint yoghourt
toes	

Cut the meat into chops and trim off excess fat. Brown the chops in the butter on both sides and remove from pan. Fry onions, then add tomatoes, paprika, parsley, salt and pepper. Put the chops and onion mixture in a casserole, cover with a tight lid and cook in oven 375 °F. (Reg. 5) for 1½–2 hours. Stir in yoghourt just before serving and return to oven for a few minutes to reheat.

114. Moussaka

1 lb. minced lamb	sea salt and black pepper
1 large onion finely chopped	2 tbs. tomato paste
2 cloves garlic finely chopped	6 tbs. stock
4 tbs. olive oil	4 unpeeled aubergines
½ lb. sliced mushrooms	2 oz. wholewheat flour
4 tomatoes peeled and sliced	2 oz. olive oil
2 tbs. chopped parsley	6 tbs. parmesan cheese

Fry onions and garlic in olive oil, add lamb and continue cooking stirring all the time until brown. Add mushrooms, tomatoes, parsley and salt and pepper to taste. Cook until onions are tender. Dilute the tomato paste with stock and add to meat mixture; simmer for 10 minutes. Slice unpeeled aubergines lengthwise; dust with flour and fry on both sides in hot olive oil. Drain well on greaseproof paper and then line a baking dish with them. Spread a layer of meat and vegetable mixture on the top, sprinkle parmesan then another layer of aubergines and so on until the dish is full, ending with a sprinkle of parmesan. Bake in moderate oven 375 °F. (Reg. 5) for ¾ hour or until top is nicely brown.

69

115. Navarin of Mutton or Lamb

2 lb. breast of lamb or mutton
2 oz. butter
3 sliced onions
1 dsp. wholewheat flour
1 bouquet garni
1 pint stock or water
sea salt and pepper

1 chopped clove garlic
2 oz. tomato paste
2 sliced carrots
2 sliced turnips
1 lb. peeled and chopped potatoes

Cut meat into pieces and brown in a little fat together with the onions. Stir in the flour, add enough water or stock to cover, then the bouquet garni, sea salt and pepper, garlic and tomato paste and bring to the boil. Simmer gently for 1½ hours. Fry carrots, turnips and potatoes and add to stew ¾ hour before the end of the cooking time. Skim off the fat, remove the bouquet garni and serve.

116. Noisettes of Lamb with Mushrooms

4 loin chops of lamb
2 oz. salted wholewheat flour
2 oz. butter
1 onion finely chopped

¾ lb. sliced mushrooms
sea salt and pepper
1 tbs. chopped parsley

Ask the butcher to bone 4 loin chops for you then roll them up to make four nice noisettes and tie them well. Dip meat in seasoned wholewheat flour and brown them in butter on both sides. Place in buttered casserole dish. Fry onion and add to casserole, add mushrooms, parsley, sea salt and pepper and any butter remaining in the pan. Cover and cook in slow oven 325 °F. (Reg. 3) for 1 hour. Serve with juices from the casserole, surrounded by creamed potatoes.

5-Poultry Dishes

Chicken
117. East Indies Chicken
118. Chicken Casserole
119. Tarragon Chicken
120. Spanish Chicken
121. Chicken Quenelles
122. Chicken Mayonnaise
123. Chicken Creams
124. Chicken Croquettes
125. Chicken Goulash
126. Coq Au Vin
127. Chicken Mould
128. Chicken Marengo
129. Portuguese Chicken
130. Fried Chicken with
    Crispy Noodles
131. Chinese Chicken with
    Walnuts

132. Chicken Risotto
133. Chicken in Aspic

Turkey
134. South American
    Fried Turkey
135. Devilled Turkey
136. Turkey Fricassee and
    Rice
137. Turkey Mould
138. Turkey Fritters
139. Turkey Pancakes

Duck
140. Salmi of Duck
141. Duck Casserole
142. Creole Duck

117. East Indies Chicken

1 medium roasting chicken	sea salt and pepper
6 oz. butter	1 teasp. curry powder
1 stick of celery	1 oz. wholewheat flour
2 onions	$\frac{1}{2}$ pint stock
2 strips of orange peel	3 tbs. cream

Melt the butter in a heavy saucepan and brown the chicken all over. Put the bird in a casserole breast downwards. Chop celery, onions and orange peel and fry in the butter, then add to the casserole well seasoned with sea salt and pepper. Mix the flour, curry powder and stock to a smooth cream and stir it into the vegetable mixture round the chicken. Put on the lid and cook in oven 350 °F. (Reg. 4) for $1\frac{1}{2}$ hours. Turn the chicken over after 45 minutes of cooking time. Pour the cream over the chicken just before serving.

118. Chicken Casserole

3 lb. chicken	2 oz. finely chopped parsley
2 tbs. butter	
2 tbs. olive oil	*Sauce*
2 chopped shallots	2 egg yolks
2 chopped carrots	$\frac{1}{4}$ pint double cream
6 coriander seeds	$\frac{1}{4}$ lb. sliced mushrooms
2 tbs. chopped parsley	juice of $\frac{1}{2}$ lemon
1 finely chopped clove garlic	peel of $\frac{1}{2}$ lemon cut in strips
$\frac{1}{4}$ teasp. powdered saffron	2 tbs. butter
sea salt and pepper	2 tbs. wholewheat flour
	2 teasp. barbados sugar

Melt butter and oil in a heatproof casserole and fry the shallots and carrots until they soften. Cut chicken into serving pieces and place on top of vegetables; add coriander seeds, parsley, garlic and saffron and just enough boiling water to half cover the chicken. Bring to the boil again, season well with sea salt and pepper, cover casserole and simmer for about 1 hour or until the chicken is cooked. Remove chicken pieces and keep warm.

Reduce the sauce over a high heat to half its original quantity. Combine egg yolks, cream, sliced mushrooms, lemon juice and lemon rind in a bowl. Melt butter in the top of a double saucepan, stir in the flour then the sauce from the casserole. Add caramelized sugar (made by browning the sugar with a little water) and simmer sauce over boiling water until smooth. Add egg and cream mixture and whisk over boiling water until thick. Do not let sauce boil or it will curdle.

Place chicken pieces back in the casserole and cover them with the sauce. Garnish with the chopped parsley.

119. Tarragon Chicken

3 lb. roasting chicken	sea salt and black pepper
large bunch fresh tarragon	1 pint double cream
½ pint water or chicken stock	

Put bunch of tarragon inside young chicken and place in large saucepan. Add ½ pint water or chicken stock, together with the giblets and sea salt and pepper to taste. Cover and cook gently for about 40 minutes until chicken is tender. Remove the bird but return the tarragon to the stock with the giblets and add 1 pint of double cream. Cook gently whisking all the time until the sauce thickens, simmer a few minutes longer. Place chicken on serving dish and pour over the sieved sauce.

120. Spanish Chicken

3 lb. roasting chicken	½ lb. peeled and sliced toma-
2 oz. chopped ham	toes
1 sliced onion	1 bouquet garni
2 cloves of garlic	sea salt and pepper
olive oil	chicken stock
3 sliced aubergines	1 wineglass dry sherry
3 sliced green peppers	

Cut chicken into pieces and brown in olive oil, remove and place in casserole. Sauté the vegetables in the oil until soft then add to casserole. Season well with sea salt and pepper, add bouquet garni and cover chicken with stock. Cover with lid and cook in oven 350 °F. (Reg. 4) for about 1 hour until chicken is tender. Before serving remove the bouquet garni and add chopped ham and a wineglassful of dry sherry. Return to oven until the gravy has boiled and serve with natural brown rice.

121. Chicken Quenelles

½ lb. raw chicken
½ lb. raw veal
3 tbs. wholewheat bread-
   crumbs
3 eggs
2 teasp. sea salt, pinch of
   pepper

½ pint single cream
2 pints chicken stock
1 tbs. wholewheat flour
juice of ½ lemon
1 teasp. barbados sugar

Mince meat three times. Soften breadcrumbs with a little cream and add to meat. Stir in a little more cream, two eggs, sea salt and pepper. Roll into balls and boil in stock for 15 minutes. Remove quenelles and keep warm. Mix flour to a smooth paste with water, add to stock, boil for 3 minutes then add rest of cream, one egg yolk, lemon juice and sugar. Pour sauce over quenelles. Serve with creamed potatoes.

122. Chicken Mayonnaise

1 cold cooked chicken
¼ lb. cold cooked french beans
¼ lb. cold cooked peas
3 diced cold cooked carrots
6 oz. salad cream or mayonnaise (see page 11)
sea salt

1 lb. natural brown rice
   cooked in seasoned chicken
   stock and cooled
½ lb. sliced tomatoes
2 hard-boiled eggs
2 oz. chopped parsley

Dice cold cooked chicken and mix with beans, peas and carrots. Add to rice, season well and mix with mayonnaise.

Garnish with sliced tomatoes, hard-boiled eggs and sprinkle with chopped parsley.

123. Chicken Creams

½ lb. cold cooked chicken	1 egg
2 oz. butter	1 dsp. lemon juice
1 finely chopped onion	¼ oz. gelatine
2 oz. wholewheat flour	4 tbs. dry cider
sea salt and pepper	¼ pint aspic jelly
¼ pint chicken stock	2 hard-boiled eggs, sliced
¼ pint milk	1 bundle watercress

Chop the chicken into small pieces. Fry the onion gently in the butter then add the flour, seasoning, half the stock and all the milk. Stir until boiling and simmer for a few minutes. Mix in the beaten egg, lemon juice and chicken, then add the gelatine dissolved in the remaining hot stock. Leave to cool, then add the cider. Rinse out 8 or 10 small moulds with cold water. Coat the bottom of each with a thin layer of aspic jelly. Leave to set, then arrange the slices of hard-boiled egg in each mould covering them first with jelly. Coat the sides with aspic jelly then fill the moulds with the chicken mixture. Allow to get firm then turn out on to individual plates and decorate with watercress.

124. Chicken Croquettes

½ lb. cold minced chicken	1 teasp. lemon juice
2 oz. butter	1 egg yolk
2 oz. finely chopped onion	sea salt and pepper
2 oz. sliced mushrooms	egg and wholewheat bread-
1 oz. wholewheat flour	crumbs, for coating
½ pint stock	vegetable oil for frying

Gently fry the onion and mushrooms in the butter, add flour and seasoning and cook for a few minutes. Stir in the hot stock and simmer for 3 minutes. Mix in the lemon juice, egg yolk

75

and chicken. Divide into small croquettes, coat in egg and wholewheat breadcrumbs and fry in deep vegetable oil.

125. Chicken Goulash

4 lb. roasting chicken	½ lb. tomatoes
4 oz. butter	1 green pepper
4 oz. onions	sea salt and pepper
½ oz. paprika powder	1 tbs. wholewheat flour
water or stock	½ pint sour cream

Cut the chicken into pieces. Fry the onions in the butter, add the paprika and a little water or stock. Put the pieces of chicken in the pan together with the sliced tomatoes and the sliced green pepper. Add seasoning and a very little stock. Cover tightly and simmer gently until the meat is tender. Add more stock if necessary. Whip up the sour cream with the flour until smooth and add this to the chicken mixture 10 minutes before it has finished cooking and bring to the boil. Serve with creamed potatoes or natural brown rice.

126. Coq au Vin

4 lb. roasting chicken	5 oz. double cream
¼ lb. sliced onions	2 tbs. vegetable oil
¼ lb. sliced mushrooms	1 oz. butter
4 oz. slice of gammon	1 oz. wholewheat flour
½ bottle red wine	sea salt, paprika and pepper
1 small glass of brandy	

Heat oil and butter and gently fry the onions, mushrooms and the diced lightly floured gammon. After a few minutes remove ingredients and place them in a casserole. Cut the chicken into pieces, dredge with well-seasoned flour, including the paprika powder, and brown the pieces in the same fat. When they are brown all over, lower the flame and add the brandy. Ignite it and allow it to burn out. Add the wine, stir the pan well and pour contents into the casserole. Cover with a lid and cook in oven 350 °F. (Reg. 4) for 1½–2 hours.

127. Chicken Mould

8 oz. cooked chicken
4 oz. natural brown rice
½ pint milk
½ pint chicken stock
1 rasher cooked bacon

½ lb. sliced mushrooms
1 teasp. chopped parsley
sea salt and pepper
2 tomatoes for a garnish

Cook the rice in a double saucepan in the stock and milk until all the liquid is absorbed. Chop the chicken, bacon and mushrooms and add them to the rice. Add parsley and seasoning, pour into rinsed mould and allow to set. Garnish with slices of tomato.

128. Chicken Marengo

3 lb. roasting chicken
6 oz. olive oil
1 lb. skinned and sliced tomatoes
1 large aubergine
2 oz. seasoned wholewheat flour

1 clove of garlic
1 teasp. tomato purée
6 oz. white wine
4 oz. hot water
sea salt and pepper
1 tbs. chopped parsley

Cut the chicken into 6 or 8 pieces and fry gently in olive oil. Cover pan and leave to simmer for 30 minutes. Slice the aubergine, dip the slices in the seasoned flour and fry gently in a little olive oil. Add the sliced tomatoes and crushed clove of garlic then the white wine. Mix the tomato purée with the hot water and add to the mixture. Season well and boil hard stirring all the time. Place the cooked chicken pieces on the serving dish and pour the sauce over them. Sprinkle with chopped parsley.

129. Portuguese Chicken

1 lb. cooked and diced chicken   a dash of brandy
½ lb. sliced mushrooms   2 egg yolks
2 oz. butter   4 oz. double cream
1 clove garlic   sea salt and pepper
1 glass sherry

Melt butter in a saucepan and sauté the diced chicken. Put chicken in serving dish and keep warm. Fry the sliced mushrooms and garlic in the same fat then add to the chicken. Pour the fat from the pan and swill with sherry and then the brandy. Allow to reduce, then add the cream, reduce a little more, then remove from the heat. Whip in the two egg yolks, add seasoning, strain and pour over the chicken mixture.

Serve with natural brown rice mixed with cooked peas and shredded pimento.

130. Fried Chicken with Crispy Noodles

½ lb. egg noodles   ¼ lb. diced cooked chicken
½ lb. lard   1 tbs. soya sauce
¼ lb. bean sprouts or 4 oz. peas   2 oz. butter
¼ lb. sliced celery   sea salt and pepper

Boil the noodles for about 5 minutes, wash and drain them well. Melt the lard in a saucepan, put the noodles in a strainer and fry in the lard until they are crisp and brown. Gently fry the chicken and vegetables in the butter, mix in the soya sauce and seasoning and serve on top of the noodles.

131. Chinese Chicken with Walnuts

½ lb. diced chicken   2 teasp. cornflour
½ lb. sliced mushrooms   1 teasp. sea salt
4 oz. walnuts   ½ teasp. barbados sugar
3 tbs. soya sauce   vegetable oil

78

Fry chicken in 3 tbs. hot oil for about 2 minutes, stirring all the time. Mix the cornflour, sugar, salt and soya sauce together and pour on top of chicken in the frying pan. Add the sliced mushrooms and cook mixture for about 5 minutes stirring constantly. Fry the walnuts in deep oil for a few minutes and mix with chicken mixture just before serving.

132. Chicken Risotto

3 lb. chicken	sea salt and pepper
1 onion	2 oz. chopped parsley
4 oz. mushrooms	1 sliced red pepper
2 oz. butter	$\frac{1}{2}$ lb. tomatoes, peeled and
8 oz. natural brown rice	chopped
1$\frac{1}{2}$ pints chicken stock	

Roast or boil the chicken for about 1 hour, cool and remove meat from bones and dice. Peel and slice the onion and the mushrooms then fry them gently in the butter in a large heavy frying pan until lightly browned. Add the rice and fry gently for 5 minutes. Pour on the boiling stock and add the sea salt and pepper. Cover and cook gently until all the stock is absorbed and the rice tender, approx. 1 hour. Add the diced chicken, the sliced pepper, the peeled and chopped tomatoes and the parsley about 10 minutes before the end of the cooking time.

133. Chicken in Aspic

$\frac{1}{2}$ lb. cold cooked diced chicken	sea salt and pepper
2 hard-boiled eggs	1 pint chicken stock
$\frac{1}{4}$ lb. cooked chopped ham	$\frac{3}{4}$ oz. gelatine
a pinch grated nutmeg	1 tbs. sherry
	watercress or lettuce

Place the diced chicken and ham at the bottom of a wetted mould with the slices of hard-boiled egg on top. Add nutmeg, salt and pepper. Melt the gelatine in the hot stock then add the sherry, mix well and pour over the chicken mixture. Leave to set and turn out on to a cold dish. Surround with watercress or lettuce leaves.

134. South American Fried Turkey

½ lb. cooked breast of turkey
2 oz. butter
½ teasp. chilli powder
1 tbs. desiccated coconut
sea salt and pepper
2 oz. wholewheat flour

egg and wholewheat bread-crumbs for coating
fat for frying
½ lb. natural brown rice
curry sauce
1 banana
3 slices pineapple

Cut turkey breast into thin slices. Mix butter, chilli powder, coconut and seasoning together and spread on each slice of turkey. Roll up and secure with a cocktail stick or clove. Dip in flour, then in egg and breadcrumbs and fry in hot fat for 5 minutes. Serve on natural brown rice with a curry sauce and slices of fried banana and pineapple.

135. Devilled Turkey

2 lb. diced cooked turkey
1 oz. butter
1 tbs. vegetable oil
1 sliced green pepper
4 oz. sliced mushrooms
4 tbs. dry white wine
2 tbs. sauce diable

½ pint turkey stock
1 tbs. wholewheat flour
1 clove garlic or pinch of garlic powder
sea salt and pepper
5 oz. single cream

Sauté sliced pepper, mushrooms and garlic in butter and oil for a few minutes. Stir in wine, sauce diable and stock. Bring to the boil and pour over the turkey pieces. Place in casserole, cover and cook in oven 375 °F. (Reg. 5) for 1 hour. Mix flour to a smooth paste with cold stock and add to the casserole, add the cream and return to the oven for a further 10 minutes. Serve with natural brown rice.

136. Turkey Fricassee and Rice

1 lb. cold diced turkey	4 oz. mushrooms
1½ oz. butter	½ a small lemon
1 oz. wholewheat flour	1 egg yolk
1 pint turkey stock	3 tbs. cream
sea salt, pepper, pinch grated nutmeg	natural brown rice

Make a sauce with the butter, flour, stock, seasoning and nutmeg. Cook the mushrooms in the lemon juice and a little stock and add to the sauce. Mix in the turkey pieces and heat through but do not boil. Mix the beaten egg yolk and the cream together, add a tbs. of the sauce, mix well and add to the turkey mixture in the saucepan. Continue cooking gently without boiling until the sauce thickens. Serve with natural brown rice.

137. Turkey Mould

1 lb. turkey scraps	½ lb. mushrooms
¼ lb. left over stuffing	2 onions
½ lb. natural brown rice cooked in turkey stock	4 oz. butter
	sea salt and pepper

Slice onions and mushrooms and fry gently in butter. Mix the cooked natural rice with the turkey scraps and stuffing, moisten with turkey stock and then mix well with the mushrooms and onions together with the butter they were cooked in. Oil a mould, pour in the well-seasoned mixture, cover with foil and steam for 1 hour. Serve with creamy tomato sauce.

138. Turkey Fritters

1 lb. turkey scraps	sea salt and pepper
2 oz. butter	1 lb. cooked mashed potatoes
1 sliced onion	egg and wholewheat bread-
¼ lb. chopped ham or bacon	crumbs for coating
1 dsp. chopped parsley	vegetable oil for deep frying

Gently fry the sliced onion in a little butter. Mix the turkey, ham and parsley then stir in the onions. Season well, and cover spoonfuls of this mixture with mashed potatoes. Brush with beaten egg, coat with wholewheat breadcrumbs and deep fry in vegetable oil.

139. Turkey Pancakes

¼ lb. wholewheat flour
sea salt
1 egg
½ pint milk

Filling
8 oz. minced cooked turkey
4 oz. sliced mushrooms

1 oz. butter
1 oz. wholewheat flour
½ pint milk
sea salt and pepper
2 tbs. cream
1 egg yolk
dash of paprika

Make the batter by beating the seasoned wholewheat flour with the egg and milk for 10 minutes. Make eight small pancakes and keep warm.

Melt the butter in a thick pan, stir in the wholewheat flour and then the warm milk, cook gently for 3 minutes until boiling; add sea salt and pepper then the cream. Cook for a further minute. Cook the sliced mushrooms in a little butter and add to minced turkey; season well, add egg yolk and a dash of paprika, then stir in the white sauce. Fill each pancake with this mixture, roll up and serve at once.

140. Salmi of Duck

1 duck
1 oz. butter
1 onion
¼ lb. sliced mushrooms
sprig of thyme and parsley

1 tomato, peeled and sliced
1 tbs. wholewheat flour
1 wineglass of port
1 teasp. Marmite
sea salt and pepper

Roast duck in oven 350 °F. (Reg. 4) allowing 25 minutes to the pound and 25 minutes over. Cut into four portions and keep warm.

Slice and gently fry the onion and the mushrooms in a little butter. Add the peeled and sliced tomato, the chopped thyme and parsley, sea salt and pepper. Cover and cook gently for 10 minutes; then add the flour, sprinkling it in and stirring well, the port wine, the Marmite and ¾ pint stock or water. Bring to the boil, skim well, and continue to cook for a further 15 minutes.

Pour this sauce over the duck portions and serve with creamed potatoes and new peas.

141. Duck Casserole

3 lb. duck	1 sliced leek
5 tbs. olive oil	1 sliced stick of celery
¼ lb. bacon rashers	1 sprig of thyme
½ lb. sliced onions	dash of paprika
1 oz. wholewheat flour	½ teasp. barbados sugar
sea salt and pepper	1 sliced orange
1½ pints vegetable stock	2 tbs. redcurrant jelly
2 tbs. white wine	

Sauté chopped bacon rashers and onions in the oil. Brown duck on all sides in same pan, sprinkle with flour and seasoning and turn into casserole. Pour in white wine and stock; add the leek, celery, paprika pepper, thyme and sugar. Cover the casserole with a tight-fitting lid and cook in centre of oven 350 °F. (Reg. 4) for 1½ hours until the duck is cooked. Place the orange slices over the breast of the duck 15 minutes before the end of the cooking time. Lift duck on to serving dish and keep warm. Skim off excess fat and reduce sauce by fast boiling in a pan. Stir in redcurrant jelly and strain sauce over duck.

142. Creole Duck

1 lb. diced cooked duck	2 tbs. chopped parsley
2 oz. butter	sea salt, pepper, paprika
1 tbs. wholewheat flour	1 pint stock or consommé
½ lb. chopped ham	1 clove
2 minced onions	¼ teasp. mace
1 sliced green pepper	4 oz. mushrooms
2 sticks chopped celery	

Melt the butter, stir in the wholewheat flour and add the chopped ham, green pepper, onion, celery, parsley, sea salt, pepper and paprika. Stir for a few minutes then add the stock or consommé, clove and mace. Simmer for 1 hour, strain and stir in the diced duck. Serve with natural brown rice and sliced sautéed mushrooms.

6-Vegetables and Salads

Vegetables

143. Garlic Stuffed Onions
144. Leeks in Wine Sauce
145. Stuffed Cabbage
146. Red Cabbage
147. Vegetable Pot Pourri
148. Braised Celery
149. Stuffed Artichokes
150. Courgettes
151. Casserole of
    Vegetables
152. Stuffed Avocado
    Pears
153. Stuffed Aubergines
154. Stuffed Green
    Peppers
155. Cheese Peppers
156. Stuffed Tomatoes
157. Green Beans in
    Savoury Sauce
158. Ratatouille
159. Vegetable and Fish
    Ragout
160. French Baked
    Potatoes
161. Pease Pudding
162. Braised Cucumber
163. Eastern Aubergines
164. Greek Mushrooms
165. Orange Beetroot

Salads

166. Wholefood Special
167. Potato Salad
168. Spanish Salad
169. Raw Vegetable Salad
170. Lettuce Salad
171. Cauliflower Salad
172. Tomato Salad
173. Green Salad
174. Salade Niçoise
175. Beetroot Salad
176. Cucumber Salad
177. Russian Salad
178. Chicory Salad
179. Banana and Walnut
    Salad
180. Celery Salad
181. Celery and Egg Salad
182. French Pepper Salad
    with Herb Dressing
183. Rice Salad
184. French Bean Salad
185. Irish Salad
186. Courgette and
    Tomato Salad
187. Courgette Salad
188. Celery and Almond
    Salad

143. Garlic Stuffed Onions

6 large onions
12 cloves garlic
1 tbs. olive oil
6 tbs. chopped parsley

3 tbs. fresh wholewheat
  breadcrumbs
sea salt and pepper to taste
4 oz. butter

Simmer onions and garlic in boiling salted water until tender. Remove and scoop out the onion centres. Mix this flesh with the finely chopped garlic and mix together with the parsley, breadcrumbs, sea salt, pepper and olive oil until smooth. Stuff the onions with this mixture; place on a greased baking dish, dot onions with butter and cook in oven 350 °F. (Reg. 4) until hot right through.

144. Leeks in Wine Sauce

2 lb. leeks
6 oz. olive oil

$\frac{1}{2}$ pint red wine

Wash the leeks well and remove the outside leaves and the roots. If they are on the large side slice them. Heat the oil in a pan, add the leeks and cook for a few minutes. Add the wine and bring to boiling point, cover and cook for 10 minutes. Remove the leeks and put in the serving dish. Continue to boil the sauce until it is thick then pour it over the leeks.

145. Stuffed Cabbage

2 small white cabbages
6 oz. minced lamb
2 oz. minced bacon
$\frac{1}{2}$ lb. chopped mushrooms
1 beaten egg
4 cloves of garlic chopped
  small

$\frac{1}{2}$ lb. wholewheat breadcrumbs
1 teasp. each of marjoram, sea
  salt, pepper, parsley
1 pinch nutmeg

Blanch the cabbages by putting them in boiling salted water for a few minutes. Remove from the pan, strain and cool. Bind

86

the rest of the ingredients together with the beaten egg and tuck between the cabbage leaves. Tie up the cabbages with string and put them into separate pots, cover with stock, put on the lids and place in oven 350 °F. (Reg. 4) for 3 hours.

146. Red Cabbage

1 medium-sized red cabbage	2 small cooking apples
4 oz. dripping	2 tbs. apple cider vinegar
8 oz. sliced onion	sea salt and pepper
4 oz. raisins	

Shred the cabbage. Fry the onions in the dripping then add the red cabbage; put the lid on the saucepan and cook for about 15 minutes. Add a little water then the raisins, chopped apples, sea salt and pepper. Cook for about 1 hour then drain off the liquid, add seasoning and vinegar and serve hot or cold.

147. Vegetable Pot Pourri

2 green peppers	$\frac{1}{2}$ lb. tomatoes, peeled and sliced
1 aubergine	
2 onions	2 oz. olive oil
$\frac{3}{4}$ lb. potatoes	1 clove garlic
sea salt, cayenne pepper	$\frac{1}{2}$ pint stock
	chopped parsley

Cut onions, potatoes, aubergines and tomatoes into thick slices. De-seed and slice the green peppers. Cook the peppers and the onions in the oil for a few minutes, add aubergines and chopped garlic and stew for a further 5 minutes. Add sea salt and pepper, potatoes and tomatoes, then the stock and simmer for 20 minutes. Pour into serving dish and sprinkle with parsley.

148. Braised Celery

2 heads of celery
¼ pint brown sauce
1 oz. butter

¼ pint stock
sea salt and pepper

Wash the celery well and cut into even lengths. Melt the butter in a pan, add the celery, stock, sea salt and pepper and stew slowly for about ½ hour. Pour the brown sauce over the celery, put the lid on the saucepan and continue to cook for a further ½ hour. Arrange the celery on the serving dish, reduce the sauce by boiling it a little more, then pour it over the celery.

149. Stuffed Artichokes

4 artichokes
2 oz. chopped mushrooms
6 oz. cooked peas
4 oz. cooked prawns

2 teasp. chopped parsley
sea salt
2 teasp. mayonnaise (see page 11)

Cook the trimmed artichokes in boiling salted water until tender. Remove centre leaves and chokes and drain well. Mix the mushrooms, peas, prawns and parsley in the mayonnaise and stuff the artichokes with this mixture.

150. Courgettes

1 lb. courgettes
1 teasp. chopped parsley
1 teasp. fresh chopped tarragon
juice and rind of ½ lemon

2 bay leaves
5 teasp. olive oil
1 chopped clove garlic
4 teasp. water
sea salt and pepper

Trim and slice the courgettes. Put all the other ingredients in a saucepan and heat gently until well mixed. Add the courgettes, cover and bring to the boil. Reduce the heat and simmer for about 10 minutes, until the courgettes are tender but not overcooked. Allow mixture to cool, chill it and serve with a green salad.

151. Casserole of Vegetables

½ lb. mushrooms	2 carrots
1½ pints water	2 onions
2 rashers of bacon	2 leeks
1 lb. potatoes	6 tbs. lentils
sea salt and pepper	1 tbs. chopped parsley

Make stock by stewing mushroom stalks in water for 1 hour. Peel and slice potatoes, carrots, onions and leeks. Cut bacon into small pieces and wash lentils well. Arrange all the ingredients in layers in a large casserole, cover with the mushroom stock, season with sea salt and pepper. Place lid on casserole, cook in slow oven 325 °F. (Reg. 3) for 2½ hours.

152. Stuffed Avocado Pears

2 large ripe avocado pears	4 oz. cottage cheese
12 toasted almonds	2 tbs. cooked shrimps
2 teasp. lemon juice	1 teasp. chopped chives
sea salt and pepper	1 tbs. sour cream

Cut avocado pears in half and remove the stones. Remove the flesh and mash with cottage cheese, lemon juice, shrimps, chopped chives and seasoning. Fill the pears with the mixture and top with toasted almonds. Pour over the sour cream and chill well.

153. Stuffed Aubergines

2 large aubergines	2 tomatoes, peeled and
½ lb. minced ham	chopped
2 onions	1 green pepper, sliced
3 oz. butter	sea salt and pepper
	2 teasp. chopped parsley

Wash and dry the aubergines and cut them in half lengthwise. Scoop out most of the pulp. Chop the pulp finely and cook in a saucepan with 1 oz. butter, the tomatoes, de-seeded sliced green pepper and chopped onions. When tender, drain and mash thoroughly and mix with the minced ham, sea salt and pepper and the rest of the butter. Fill the shells with this mixture and sprinkle the parsley over the top.

154. Stuffed Green Peppers

4 green peppers	2 oz. cooked natural brown
2 oz. butter	rice
1 onion minced	1 tbs. chopped parsley
2 oz. minced pork	1 tbs. tomato purée
	sea salt and pepper

De-seed the green peppers and boil them in salted water for 5 minutes until tender. Mix onion, rice, pork, parsley, tomato purée, sea salt and pepper and stuff the peppers with this mixture. Place in casserole, dot with butter and pour over 2 tbs. water; cover with lid and cook in oven 350 °F. (Reg. 4) for ½ hour.

155. Cheese Peppers

2 large green peppers	sea salt and pepper
1 oz. butter	3 hard-boiled eggs
1 oz. plain wholewheat flour	4 oz. ham
½ pint milk	3 oz. grated cheddar cheese

Cut the peppers in half lengthwise and de-seed. Put in a pan of salted boiling water and cook for 15 minutes. Melt the butter, stir in the flour and cook over low heat for 2 minutes. Add the milk gradually, season well, bring to the boil and cook for 3 minutes stirring all the time. Chop the hard-boiled eggs and cut the ham into small cubes. Stir the eggs, ham and most of the cheese into the sauce and reheat. Fill the pepper halves, top with remaining cheese and brown under a hot grill.

156. Stuffed Tomatoes

4 large tomatoes	⅛ pint mayonnaise (see page
2 oz. cooked shrimps	11)
2 oz. cucumber	sea salt and pepper
2 hard-boiled eggs	1 crisp lettuce

Cut the tops off the tomatoes and scoop out the flesh. Chop the cucumber and the hard-boiled eggs, season well and mix with shrimps and mayonnaise and a little of the tomato pulp. Fill the tomato cases and serve on lettuce leaves.

157. Green Beans in Savoury Sauce

1 lb. french or runner beans	1½ oz. wholewheat flour
1 chopped onion	½ pint milk
2 oz. butter	sea salt and pepper
1 tbs. olive oil	1 clove garlic
2 tbs. chopped parsley	¼ teasp. grated nutmeg

Leave the french beans whole, just string if necessary; slice the runner beans. Cook in boiling salted water for 10 minutes until tender. Melt butter with the olive oil, stir in the parsley, the crushed garlic and the chopped onion, fry gently for 2 minutes. Stir in the flour and gradually add the milk; add the nutmeg, season well and boil for 3 minutes. Add the beans, heat through and serve.

158. Ratatouille

4 oz. olive oil	2 baby marrows
2 onions	4 peeled tomatoes
2 green peppers	sea salt and pepper
2 aubergines	1 tbs. chopped parsley
pinch marjoram, pinch of basil	2 cloves garlic

Slice onions and baby marrows; chop peppers, tomatoes and aubergines. Sauté onions in olive oil, add peppers and auber-

gines and a few minutes later the tomatoes and marrows.
Gently stew the vegetables in a covered pan for 30 minutes.
Add sea salt and pepper, herbs and crushed garlic; cook un-
covered for 10 minutes until vegetables are all well mixed.
Serve hot or cold.

159. Vegetable and Fish Ragout

4 oz. tuna fish	¼ pint tomato purée
4 aubergines	2 tbs. barbados sugar
4 oz. olive oil	sea salt and pepper
3 anchovy fillets	¼ pint apple cider vinegar
1 head of celery	1½ oz. capers
1 onion	2 tbs. chopped parsley
4 oz. black olives	

Peel and slice the aubergines, sprinkle them with sea salt and
leave for 1 hour. Drain well and fry gently in the olive oil. Soak
the anchovies in warm water, blanch and chop the celery, slice
the onion and stone the olives. Cook the sliced onion in some
olive oil, stir in the tomato purée and the barbados sugar. Cook
until the mixture is dark and thick; stir in the vinegar. Simmer
for a few minutes then stir in the celery, olives, aubergines,
capers and the diced anchovies. Cook for a further few minutes
then add the tuna fish, parsley, sea salt and pepper. Cool and
then chill before serving.

160. French Baked Potatoes

1½ lb. potatoes	sea salt and black pepper
3 oz. butter	1 clove garlic
½ pint milk	

Grease a fireproof dish with butter and rub with garlic. Cut
the potatoes in thin slices and arrange them in layers in the
dish. Season between the layers with sea salt and black pepper.
Pour on the milk, dot with butter and bake in oven 400 °F.
(Reg. 6) for 1 hour.

161. Pease Pudding

1 lb. dried peas
6 bacon rinds
½ pint single cream

sea salt, black pepper
celery salt
3 oz. butter

Soak dried peas overnight. Simmer in water containing the bacon rinds for 1 hour. Sieve the peas whilst hot, add the single cream and season with celery salt, sea salt and black pepper; stir in the butter and serve.

162. Braised Cucumber

3 small cucumbers
1 chopped onion

1 oz. butter
pinch barbados sugar

Melt the butter in a saucepan, fry the onion gently, then add the sugar and the diced cucumber. Put the lid on the pan and simmer for ½ hour.

163. Eastern Aubergines

2 large aubergines
2 large green peppers
2 tbs. chopped mint
6 tbs. apple cider vinegar

sea salt and pepper
½ pint tomato juice
olive oil for frying

Slice aubergines fairly thickly and soak in salt water for 1 hour. De-seed and slice the green peppers. Cook aubergines and peppers in olive oil until tender. Remove from oil and place some at the bottom of the serving dish, sprinkle with sea salt, pepper, mint and apple cider vinegar and repeat in layers until dish is full. Pour over the tomato juice and chill.

164. Greek Mushrooms

1 lb. small mushrooms	sea salt and peppercorns
2 carrots	1 bouquet garni
1 onion	1 clove garlic
1 tbs. corn oil	$\frac{1}{2}$ lb. tomatoes
4 tbs. olive oil	2 tbs. chopped parsley
4 oz. white wine	

Put olive oil and corn oil in the pan and sauté the sliced carrots and the sliced onion until they are tender. Add a little wine, sea salt and the crushed peppercorns to taste, a large bouquet garni and the crushed clove of garlic. Slice the washed mushrooms, peel and slice the tomatoes and add to the vegetables with a little more wine if necessary. Cook uncovered for 20 minutes. Remove from the heat, allow to cool, and remove the herbs. Place in serving dish and sprinkle with chopped parsley.

165. Orange Beetroot

6 small cooked beetroots	$\frac{3}{4}$ pint orange juice
2 oz. butter	rind of 2 oranges
2 oz. wholewheat flour	sea salt and pepper
$\frac{3}{4}$ pint water	2 teasp. barbados sugar

Melt the butter in a pan, stir in the flour, then slowly add the water stirring all the time. Add the orange juice, rind, salt, pepper and sugar. Stir until the sauce thickens. Slice the cooked beetroots and stir into the sauce.

166. Wholefood Special Salad

¼ lb. washed sliced carrots
½ head celery, washed and sliced
¼ dutch cabbage, washed and shredded
1 skinned and washed raw beetroot
½ lb. washed and chopped tomatoes
1 green pepper, washed, de-seeded and sliced

¼ onion, chopped small
1 chopped washed unpeeled apple
2 oz. chopped nuts

Dressing
1 oz. apple cider vinegar
3 oz. safflower oil
sea salt, pepper
pinch garlic powder, barbados sugar

167. Potato Salad

1 lb. potatoes
2 oz. chopped onions
5 oz. mayonnaise (see page 11)

1 oz. chopped parsley
sea salt and pepper

Boil potatoes, cool and chop into small cubes. Sprinkle in the chopped parsley and the onions, mix all the ingredients with mayonnaise and season well.

168. Spanish Salad

1 lb. tomatoes
2 sliced onions
2 sliced green peppers

1 oz. vegetable oil
½ oz. apple cider vinegar
1 clove garlic
sea salt, pepper

Wash and slice tomatoes, onions and peppers having first removed the pepper seeds and pith. Chop the garlic and mix all ingredients in the vinegar and oil; season well.

169. Raw Vegetable Salad

$\frac{1}{2}$ head of celery
$\frac{1}{4}$ lb. carrots
$\frac{1}{4}$ lb. tomatoes
$\frac{1}{4}$ cucumber

$\frac{1}{4}$ dutch cabbage
1 oz. vegetable oil
$\frac{1}{2}$ oz. apple cider vinegar
garlic salt, sea salt, pepper

Wash all the vegetables, chop small and toss in dressing. Season well.

170. Lettuce Salad

1 lettuce
$\frac{1}{2}$ cucumber
$\frac{1}{2}$ lb. tomatoes
$\frac{1}{2}$ lb. cooked beetroot

2 hard-boiled eggs
1 bundle radishes
mayonnaise or french dressing (see page 11)

Wash vegetables well. Arrange lettuce as the base and decorate with the other vegetables. Serve with mayonnaise or french dressing.

171. Cauliflower Salad

1 cauliflower
$\frac{1}{2}$ lb. tomatoes
1 oz. chopped parsley

sea salt, paprika
3 oz. mayonnaise (see page 11)

Break cauliflower head into spriglets, wash well. Chop tomatoes and mix with the cauliflower and chopped parsley. Mix with mayonnaise and sprinkle with paprika.

172. Tomato Salad

1 lb. tomatoes
$\frac{1}{2}$ oz. chopped parsley
$\frac{1}{2}$ oz. chopped chives
$\frac{1}{2}$ oz. vegetable oil

$\frac{1}{4}$ oz. apple cider vinegar
garlic powder or clove of garlic
sea salt and pepper

Wash tomatoes; slice, season and sprinkle with chopped parsley and chives. Toss in french dressing (see page 11).

Vegetables and Salads

173. Green Salad

1 lettuce
1 bundle watercress
1 oz. chopped chives

½ oz. vegetable oil
¼ oz. apple cider vinegar
sea salt, pepper, clove garlic

Wash vegetables well. Rub bowl with clove of garlic and toss green vegetables in oil and vinegar dressing. Season well.

174. Salade Niçoise

1 lettuce
1 green pepper
½ lb. tomatoes
1 clove garlic
2 hard-boiled eggs
sea salt and pepper
4 oz. tuna fish
1 oz. anchovy fillets

½ lb. cooked natural brown rice
1 oz. chopped parsley
2 oz. french dressing made with apple cider vinegar and vegetable oil (see page 11)

Remove seeds and pith from green peppers, slice finely. Wash and separate lettuce. Wash and chop tomatoes. Rub large bowl with garlic and pour in the dressing. Toss peppers, lettuce, tomatoes, rice, chopped eggs, fish and parsley in the dressing and decorate with anchovy fillets.

175. Beetroot Salad

1 lb. cooked beetroot
¼ oz. caraway seeds
1 oz. chopped parsley

1 oz. vegetable oil
½ oz. apple cider vinegar
sea salt, pepper, clove garlic

Slice beetroot finely, mix with caraway seeds and oil and vinegar dressing, season well and sprinkle with chopped parsley.

176. Cucumber Salad

1 cucumber	1 plain yoghourt
½ oz. apple cider vinegar	¼ oz. barbados sugar
1 oz. chopped parsley	sea salt and paprika pepper

Make a dressing by mixing yoghourt, vinegar, sugar, sea salt and paprika. Slice cucumber finely, cover with dressing and sprinkle with parsley.

177. Russian Salad

½ lb. cooked peas	garlic powder
¼ lb. diced carrots	paprika
¼ lb. cooked diced potatoes	½ pint mayonnaise (see page
2 oz. diced cooked beetroot	11)
sea salt and pepper	

Mix all the vegetables together in a large bowl, season well, and stir in the mayonnaise.

178. Chicory Salad

2 heads of chicory	juice of 1 lemon
1 green pepper	a pinch of chopped mint
1 oz. green olives	¼ teasp. french mustard
	sea salt, pepper, garlic powder
Dressing	¼ teasp. barbados sugar
1 oz. olive oil	

Wash and slice chicory heads. Remove pith and seeds from inside green pepper and slice finely. Slice olives. Mix all ingredients together and stir in the dressing.

179. Banana and Walnut Salad

4 bananas	1 bundle watercress
juice of 1 lemon	2 oz. mayonnaise (see page
½ oz. chopped parsley	11)
2 oz. chopped walnuts	

Slice bananas into thin rounds and mix with lemon juice in a bowl. Add chopped walnuts, parsley and mayonnaise. Decorate with watercress.

180. Celery Salad

2 heads of celery
½ oz. chopped parsley

2 oz. mayonnaise (see page 11)

Wash and chop celery. Mix with mayonnaise and sprinkle with parsley.

181. Celery and Egg Salad

2 heads of celery
½ oz. chopped parsley
2 oz. mayonnaise (see page 11)

2 hard-boiled eggs
¼ chopped onion
½ oz. chopped walnuts

Wash and chop celery. Chop hard-boiled eggs. Mix with parsley, nuts and onion. Stir in the mayonnaise.

182. French Pepper Salad with Herb Dressing

1 large green pepper
1 large sweet red pepper
2 ripe tomatoes
2 hard-boiled eggs
2 oz. anchovy fillets
8 olives

Herb dressing
1 clove garlic finely chopped
1 tbs. each finely chopped parsley, tarragon, chervil and chives
4 tbs. olive oil
2 tbs. apple cider vinegar
sea salt and black pepper

Make herb dressing by mixing all the ingredients with the vinegar and oil and seasoning to taste.

Wash peppers, remove seeds and pith from inside and slice finely. Slice tomatoes and lay on bottom of the dish, sprinkle with dressing; add a layer of green pepper slices, sprinkle with dressing; add layer of red pepper slices, sprinkle with dressing.

Slice hard-boiled eggs and put a layer of egg slices over the pepper; sprinkle with dressing. Decorate with anchovy slices and olives and chill in refrigerator.

183. Rice Salad

½ lb. natural brown rice
1 hard-boiled egg
¼ lb. mushrooms
6 black olives
a few slices pimento
4 slices cucumber
1 tomato

chives chopped finely
parsley

Dressing
2 tbs. olive oil
1 tbs. apple cider vinegar
sea salt and black pepper

Boil rice for 20 minutes in a large pan of boiling salted water. Drain well, and dress with oil and vinegar whilst still warm; season well. Dice the cucumber, chop the hard-boiled egg and the tomato. Slice the pimento and the olives. Slice and sauté the mushrooms. Mix all ingredients with the dressed rice and sprinkle with chopped chives and parsley.

184. French Bean Salad

1 lb. french beans

Dressing
3 tbs. olive oil

1 tbs. apple cider vinegar
pinch of barbados sugar, sea
    salt, pepper

Chop and cook french beans. Toss in dressing in a large bowl; season well.

185. Irish Salad

1 lettuce
1 clove garlic
4 oz. cooked peas
2 oz. cooked asparagus tips
sea salt, pepper
4 oz. finely sliced raw mush-
    rooms

¼ pint shelled shrimps
4 oz. tuna fish
2 hard-boiled eggs

Dressing
4 tbs. olive oil
2 tbs. apple cider vinegar
sea salt and pepper

Wash lettuce. Rub large bowl with cut garlic clove and toss lettuce in dressing until well coated. Add the rest of the ingredients and garnish with the sliced hard-boiled eggs.

186. Courgette and Tomato Salad

1 lb. courgettes	½ pint water
¾ lb. tomatoes	1 bay leaf
2 lemons	pinch of dried thyme
1 tbs. olive oil	sea salt

Slice the courgettes thickly, sprinkle with sea salt and leave for ½ hour. Heat the olive oil, water, bay leaf and thyme to boiling point. Put the courgettes in a separate pan, cover with lemon juice then add the boiling liquid. Cook for 15 minutes then add the peeled and sliced tomatoes; cook for a further 5 minutes and allow to cool. Serve cold.

187. Courgette Salad

½ lb. courgettes thinly sliced	½ lb. chopped tomatoes
6 oz. tuna fish	2 teasp. mayonnaise (see page 11)
2 teasp. chopped parsley	
2 chopped hard-boiled eggs	2 teasp. olive oil
sea salt and pepper	1 teasp. apple cider vinegar
1 green pepper de-seeded and sliced	

Parboil the courgettes in boiling salted water for a few minutes and drain. Mix the tuna fish, hard-boiled eggs and parsley in the mayonnaise; add the courgettes. Toss the sliced peppers and tomatoes in well-seasoned oil and vinegar dressing. Place the fish mixture in the middle of a dish and surround with the peppers and tomatoes.

188. Celery and Almond Salad

1 head of celery
2 oz. asparagus tips
2 oz. blanched and chopped almonds

4 oz. mayonnaise (see page 11)
1 lettuce
sea salt and pepper

Wash and chop the celery and mix with asparagus tips and chopped almonds. Stir in the mayonnaise, season with sea salt and pepper and serve on a bed of lettuce.

7-Sweet Dishes

189. Pineapple Mousse
190. Lemon Pudding
191. Apple and Almond Sponge
192. Caramel Peaches
193. Baked Peaches
194. Chocolate Flan
195. Zabaglione
196. Rhubarb Meringue
197. Profiteroles and Chocolate Sauce
198. Caramel Cream
199. Banana Fritters
200. Pineapple Pudding
201. Orange Meringue Pudding
202. Apple and Raisin Flan
203. Date Flan
204. Chocolate Pear Flan
205. Blackcurrant Pie
206. Crispy Pancakes with Hot Chocolate Sauce
207. Curaçao Pancakes
208. Pineapple Upside-down Cake
209. Chestnut and Sultana Cream
210. Chestnut Snow
211. Raspberry Soufflé
212. Rhum Baba
213. Peach Mallows
214. Coffee Meringue Flan
215. Apricot Cream
216. Blackberry and Coconut Crunch
217. Coffee Crumble
218. Chocolate Mousse
219. Lemon Meringue Pie
220. Orange Cups
221. Lemon Soufflé
222. Peach Cream Tarts
223. Syllabub
224. Raspberry Melon
225. Rhubarb Jelly
226. Mincemeat Sponge
227. Peach Ambrosia

189. Pineapple Mousse

1 lb. pineapple pieces	juice of 2 lemons
1 tbs. powdered gelatine	pinch of sea salt
2 tbs. cold water	12 oz. tin evaporated milk
2 oz. barbados sugar	¼ pint single cream

Sprinkle gelatine on the cold water and leave to soak. Pour pineapple pieces into saucepan, add sugar and salt and gently bring to the boil. Take pan off the heat and add soaked gelatine and stir until dissolved. Add lemon juice and set on one side until beginning to thicken. Whisk evaporated milk until thick then fold in the gelatine mixture and the cream. Pour into serving dish and refrigerate until required.

190. Lemon Pudding

Juice and rind of 1 large lemon	2 oz. wholewheat self-raising
2 oz. butter or margarine	flour
3 oz. barbados sugar ·	½ pint water
2 eggs	

Cream butter, sugar and lemon rind together until creamy. Add the beaten egg yolks, and stir in alternately the water, lemon juice and flour. Fold in the stiffly beaten egg whites. Pour into a greased 1½ pint size pie-dish and bake for 40 minutes in oven 350 °F. (Reg. 4).

191. Apple and Almond Sponge

1 lb. cooking apples	1 egg
2 oz. wholewheat bread-crumbs	1½ oz. ground almonds
	3 oz. butter or margarine
3 oz. barbados sugar	

Peel, core and slice the apples, cook in a little water until soft. Stir in the breadcrumbs and pour into a greased pie-dish. Cream butter and sugar, add the beaten egg and the ground almonds. Pour over the apple mixture and bake in oven 350 °F. (Reg. 4) for 40 minutes. Serve hot or cold with cream.

192. Caramel Peaches

4 peaches	2 tbs. milk
¼ pint double cream	1 oz. butter
4 oz. barbados sugar	2 oz. chopped nuts

Stand the peaches in boiling water then drop into cold and rub gently with the fingers to remove skin. Drain and cool, then cut in half and remove stones. Fill the peach centres with whipped cream sweetened with a little barbados sugar and secure halves together with cocktail sticks. Put rest of sugar, milk and butter in a saucepan, bring to the boil and simmer for 10 minutes. Beat until beginning to thicken, then pour over peaches. When cold remove sticks and top with cream and nuts.

193. Baked Peaches

4 large peaches	pinch of powdered cinnamon
1 tbs. ground almonds	¼ pint double cream or ice-cream
1 dsp. thick honey	cream

Dip the peaches into boiling water then into cold and gently remove the skin. Cut in half and remove the stone. Place the halves in the serving dish, cut side up, and fill with a mixture of ground almonds and thick honey. Sprinkle with cinnamon and grill gently until the honey is bubbling. Serve hot or cold with cream or ice-cream.

194. Chocolate Flan

5 oz. digestive biscuits	¼ oz. powdered gelatine
1½ oz. butter	1½ oz. cooking chocolate
3 oz. barbados sugar	2 eggs
½ pint milk	1 wineglass brandy
pinch of sea salt	

Roll the digestive biscuits out into fine crumbs; add 1 teasp. barbados sugar. Melt the butter in a pan and stir in the biscuits. Line a shallow tin or pie dish with this mixture and bake for 7 minutes in oven 375 °F. (Reg. 5). Blend the milk, the rest of the sugar and the sea salt in a saucepan, add the powdered gelatine and the grated chocolate and slowly melt together. Beat up the egg yolks in a bowl and add to them a little of the cooled milk mixture; gradually stir in the remainder. Return to the heat and gently heat but do not boil. Remove and stir until thick. When cool stir in the brandy and fold in the beaten egg whites. Pour this mixture into the pie shell and chill.

195. Zabaglione

3 egg yolks   3 tbs. marsala
3 tbs. barbados sugar

Beat egg yolks and sugar together until pale and fluffy. Put into the top of a double saucepan; add slightly warmed wine. Beat over a good heat for 5 minutes until the mixture is like whipped cream. Remove from heat and continue beating for a further 2 minutes. Pour into glasses and serve hot.

196. Rhubarb Meringue

1½ lb. young rhubarb   4 oz. demerara sugar
4 oz. barbados sugar   2 eggs

Slice rhubarb and place in a casserole with barbados sugar but no water. Cover and cook in oven until tender. Allow to cool, then stir in two beaten egg yolks. Beat the egg whites with demerara sugar until stiff and pile on top. Cook in low oven for 1 hour until meringue is crisp and golden.

197. Profiteroles and Chocolate Sauce

4 oz. butter
¼ pint water
8 oz. wholewheat flour
pinch sea salt
4 eggs
½ pint double cream
1 tbs. kirsch (optional)

Sauce
6 oz. cooking chocolate
3 tbs. water
3 teasp. vegetable oil
1 oz. barbados sugar

Heat butter and water together to boiling point, add the flour and pinch of sea salt all in one go and stir hard with a wooden spoon. Beat until the mixture is smooth and creamy and leaves the side of the pan. Cool the mixture slightly, beat in the eggs one at a time and continue beating until smooth and glossy. Put mixture in small spoonfuls on a greased tray and bake in oven 350 °F. (Reg. 4) for 30 minutes. When the balls are brown, remove from oven, slit each one to allow the steam to escape and leave to cool on a wire rack.

Blend together the chocolate, water, oil and sugar in a small pan over gentle heat until the chocolate has melted and the mixture is smooth.

Whip up the cream, add a little sugar and the kirsch and fill the balls with this mixture. Place them on the serving dish and decorate them with the chocolate sauce and more whipped cream.

198. Caramel Cream

Caramel
3½ oz. demerara sugar
5 oz. cold water

Cream
4 eggs

pinch of sea salt
1 pint milk
1 teasp. vanilla essence
1 oz. barbados sugar

Make caramel by cooking demerara sugar in the cold water over a low heat until the sugar has dissolved, then boiling quickly for a few minutes until the syrup forms a ball in cold water. Turn syrup into warm soufflé dish and run it round the bottom and sides; put it on one side to set. Beat the eggs lightly, add 1 oz. barbados sugar and the pinch of sea salt and stir well until sugar is dissolved. Heat the milk and stir into egg mixture; add the vanilla essence. When the caramel mixture and the custard are cold pour the custard into the dish through a strainer. Put the dish into a baking tin, pour hot water into the baking tin up to half-way up the dish, cover and bake in oven 350 °F. (Reg. 4) for 50 minutes. When cooked remove from the oven and allow to cool. Chill if possible. Loosen round top edge and turn out on to serving dish.

N.B.—Great care must be taken when boiling barbados sugar as it burns very quickly. Lift off heat whilst boiling if necessary and use low heat throughout.

199. Banana Fritters

4 bananas	1 egg white
2 oz. plain wholewheat flour	fat for deep frying
pinch of sea salt	barbados sugar
1 dsp. olive oil	lemon wedges
$\frac{1}{8}$ pint tepid water	

Add oil and tepid water to salted flour and mix to a smooth paste. Leave for $\frac{1}{2}$ hour. Cut the bananas lengthwise and then across. Whisk the egg white stiffly and fold into the batter. Dip the bananas into the batter and deep fry. Drain and sprinkle with barbados sugar and serve with lemon wedges.

200. Pineapple Pudding

6 oz. pineapple chunks	1 pint milk
2 oz. wholewheat flour	2 eggs
2 oz. butter or margarine	3 oz. demerara sugar
2 oz. barbados sugar	

Melt the butter in a saucepan, add the flour and cook for a minute or two stirring all the time, then add the milk. Stir well and add the sugar and the pineapple chunks. Separate the whites and the yolks of the eggs; beat the yolks into the mixture and cook gently for a few minutes. Turn the mixture into a greased ovenproof dish and bake in oven 350 °F. (Reg. 4) for 20 minutes.

Beat up the egg whites with the demerara sugar until stiff, pile on top of the pudding and return to a low oven for $\frac{1}{2}$ hour or until the meringue is crisp.

201. Orange Meringue Pudding

3 oranges	3 oz. wholewheat bread-
4 eggs	crumbs
$\frac{1}{2}$ pint milk	3 oz. barbados sugar
2 oz. butter	6 oz. demerara sugar

Boil the butter in the milk and pour it over the breadcrumbs; stir in the barbados sugar and the beaten yolks of the eggs. When this mixture is cool stir in the rind and pulp of the oranges, mix well and pour into a greased ovenproof dish. Bake in oven 350 °F. (Reg. 4) for $\frac{1}{2}$ hour until set.

Beat up the egg whites with the demerara sugar, pile the meringue on top of the pudding and return to a low oven for $\frac{1}{2}$ hour or until the meringue is crisp.

202. Apple and Raisin Flan

8 oz. wholewheat flour	4 oz. barbados sugar
$3\frac{1}{2}$ oz. lard	2 oz. raisins
$3\frac{1}{2}$ oz. margarine	1 tbs. lemon juice
cold water	pinch of cinnamon
pinch of sea salt	whipped cream
1 lb. cooking apples	

Make flan by rubbing fat into salted flour, adding enough cold water to bind into a dough and rolling it out. Line deep pie-dish with pastry and bake in oven 375 °F. (Reg. 5) for 25 minutes.

Stew the cooking apples with a little water, add the sugar, the raisins, cinnamon and lemon juice. Allow to cool and pour into pastry case. Decorate with whipped cream.

203. Date Flan

8 oz. wholewheat flour	6 oz. dates
3½ oz. lard	grated rind of ½ orange
3½ oz. margarine	½ pint custard sauce
cold water	¼ pint water
pinch of sea salt	

Make flan case by rubbing fat into salted flour and mixing to stiff dough with cold water. Roll out and line flan tin with pastry. Cook in oven 375 °F. (Reg. 5) for 25 minutes.

Cook dates gently in water with the rind of ½ orange until they make a thick paste. Spread the mixture over the flan case and serve with custard sauce.

204. Chocolate Pear Flan

8 oz. wholewheat flour	1 oz. cornflour
3½ oz. lard	1 oz. plain chocolate
3½ oz. margarine	1 oz. barbados sugar
cold water	½ pint milk
pinch of sea salt	1 egg
4 fresh cooked pears halved	whipped cream

Make flan case by rubbing fat into salted flour and mixing to a stiff dough with cold water. Roll out and line flan tin with pastry. Cook in oven 375 °F. (Reg. 5) for 25 minutes. When cool place pear halves in flan case.

Blend cornflour with a little milk. Heat the remainder of the milk and pour on to cornflour. Stir and return to the heat for 3 minutes, stirring all the time. Add grated chocolate and sugar, cool a little and then add the egg yolk. Stir over heat until the chocolate melts, then cool. Beat egg whites stiffly and fold into the mixture. Pour mixture over the pears in the flan case and decorate with whipped cream.

205. Blackcurrant Pie

2 oz. butter	3 oz. barbados sugar
2 tbs. golden syrup	2 eggs
2 oz. cornflakes	½ oz. powdered gelatine
¼ pint blackcurrant purée	whipped cream

Melt the butter and syrup in a pan; add the cornflakes; mix well, then press into a flan tin and leave until firm. Mix sugar, egg yolks and purée, put into a pan over hot water and beat until thick. Dissolve the gelatine in 3 tbs. hot water and stir into the mixture. Beat the egg whites until stiff and fold into the mixture. Put flan case carefully on serving dish and fill with mixture. Decorate with whipped cream.

206. Crispy Pancakes with Hot Chocolate Sauce

4 oz. wholewheat flour	*Sauce*
pinch of sea salt	¼ pint milk
1 egg	1 tbs. cornflour
½ pint milk	1 tbs. cocoa powder
deep fat for frying	2 tbs. barbados sugar
	¼ pint cream

Beat the salted flour with the egg and milk for 5 minutes. Fry pancakes, then cut in strips and fry strips in deep fat until crisp. Serve piled up on serving dish with hot chocolate sauce.

The sauce is made by mixing together the cornflour, sugar, cocoa powder and cream, then adding the boiling milk and stirring over the heat until it thickens.

207. Curaçao Pancakes

4 oz. wholewheat flour	1 wineglass curaçao
1 egg	4 oz. thick honey
¼ pint water	¼ pint whipped cream

Make batter by beating together the flour, egg, water and curaçao. Fry pancakes and serve with thick honey and whipped cream.

208. Pineapple Upside-down Cake

Cake	*On bottom of cake tin*
4 oz. self-raising wholewheat flour	1 small pineapple skinned and cut into small pieces
2 oz. barbados sugar	4 oz. barbados sugar
4 oz. margarine or butter	3 oz. butter
2 eggs	
3 oz. boiling water	

Cream margarine and 2 oz. barbados sugar. Add the eggs, flour and boiling water. Dot the bottom of the cake tin with butter, sprinkle over it the barbados sugar and then the pineapple pieces. Pour the cake mixture over this and bake in oven 350 °F. (Reg. 4) for 40 minutes. Turn upside-down on to serving dish and serve with whipped cream.

209. Chestnut and Sultana Cream

1 lb. chestnuts	juice and rind of 1 lemon
2 teasp. olive oil	1 teasp. allspice
1 lb. seedless sultanas	small piece cinnamon
2 oz. barbados sugar	2 cloves

Stab chestnuts on their flat side then fry them in the olive oil. Skin them, cover them with salted water and cook until tender. In another pan cover the sultanas with water, add the rind and juice of the lemon, the allspice and cinnamon and simmer until water is absorbed. Add chestnuts and barbados sugar. Serve cold with cream.

210. Chestnut Snow

2 lb. chestnuts	1 wineglass brandy
½ pint milk	½ pint whipped cream
2 tbs. barbados sugar	few drops vanilla essence

Boil and remove the skins of the chestnuts. Cook them in a double saucepan with the milk, sugar and vanilla essence.

When the mixture resembles porridge, put it through a sieve on to the serving dish, pour over the brandy and top with whipped cream.

211. Raspberry Soufflé

½ lb. raspberries	2 oz. barbados sugar
½ gill cream	3 eggs
2 oz. cornflour	2 oz. wholemeal breadcrumbs

Put raspberries, cream, cornflour and sugar into a basin and pulp with a wooden spoon. Beat in the yolks of the eggs and the breadcrumbs. Stir in the lightly whipped egg whites and turn the mixture into well-greased pie-dish. Bake in oven 375 °F. (Reg. 5) for 25 minutes. Serve at once.

212. Rhum Baba

8 oz. wholewheat flour	cherries and whipped cream
½ oz. fresh yeast	for decoration
½ oz. barbados sugar	
¼ pint milk	*Syrup*
2 eggs	4 oz. demerara sugar
3 oz. melted butter	1 tbs. rum
sea salt	5 oz. water

Cream the yeast and the sugar together and add the lukewarm milk. Mix well and add to the salted flour. Add the beaten eggs and the melted butter. Mix and beat with the hands for several minutes. Cover and leave the dough to double in size in a warm place, about 40 minutes. Beat again and pour into large buttered ring-mould. Leave to prove for 10 minutes. Bake in hot oven 425 °F. (Reg. 7) for 25 minutes, then turn out carefully.

Make syrup by boiling sugar slowly in the water. N.B.— Great care must be taken when boiling barbados sugar as it burns very easily. Cool a little and stir in the rum. Pour the syrup over the cake while the cake is still warm, fill the middle with whipped cream and decorate with cherries.

213. Peach Mallows

8 fresh peaches
3 oz. butter
8 marshmallows

3 tbs. desiccated coconut
pinch of cinnamon

Skin peaches after dipping them in boiling water, halve and remove stones. Place peach halves in patty tins, sprinkle with cinnamon, cover with melted butter and heat in oven. Whilst hot cover with sliced marshmallows, sprinkle with coconut and heat under the grill.

214. Coffee Meringue Flan

6 oz. wholewheat flour
2½ oz. lard
2½ oz. margarine
water
pinch sea salt

Filling
1 oz. cornflour
½ pint milk

2 oz. barbados sugar
2 egg yolks
1 oz. butter
1 tbs. coffee essence

Meringue
2 egg whites
3 oz. demerara sugar
a little grated chocolate

Make the flan case by rubbing the fat into the flour and mixing to a dough with cold water. Roll out and line an ovenproof shallow dish with pastry. Bake blind in oven 325 °F. (Reg. 3) for 15 minutes.

Blend the cornflour with a little cold milk. Heat the remaining milk and when almost boiling stir in the blended cornflour. Boil for a few minutes then add the sugar, butter and coffee essence. Remove from heat and add egg yolks. Pour into the pastry shell.

Whisk up the egg whites with the demerara sugar. Pile the meringue on top of the coffee filling and bake in oven 300 °F. (Reg. 2) until the meringue is crisp. When cold sprinkle with grated chocolate.

Sweet Dishes

215. Apricot Cream

12 oz. cooked fresh apricots
1 dsp. powdered gelatine
1 tbs. warm water
1 gill cream
1 gill milk

2 oz. barbados sugar
few drops almond essence
1 tbs. cointreau
whipped cream

Dissolve the gelatine in the warm water. Pulp the apricots and add the gelatine. Fold in the lightly whipped cream flavoured with almond essence and sweetened to taste, then add the milk. Add the cointreau and pour mixture into glass dishes. Decorate with whipped cream and chill well.

216. Blackberry and Coconut Crunch

½ lb. blackberries
4 oz. margarine
4 oz. barbados sugar

4 oz. desiccated coconut
4 oz. wholewheat flour

Put the blackberries in a pie-dish, sprinkle with sugar. Rub the margarine into the flour, sugar and coconut and spread on top of the blackberries. Cook in oven 375 °F. (Reg. 5) for 40 minutes.

217. Coffee Crumble

1 dsp. wholewheat flour
2 dsp. cornflour
1 teasp. cocoa powder
½ pint milk
½ pint black coffee
3 oz. barbados sugar

2 oz. margarine
4 oz. wholewheat browned breadcrumbs
4 oz. quick-cooking porridge oats

Mix flour, cornflour and cocoa together with a little milk. Heat the rest of the milk and the black coffee together. Pour on to blended cornflour, return to pan and boil for 5 minutes. Add 2 oz. sugar and pour into fireproof dish. Rub margarine into crumbs, oats and rest of sugar. Spread on top of coffee mixture and bake in oven 400 °F. (Reg. 6) for 15 minutes.

218. Chocolate Mousse

3 oz. plain chocolate	2 eggs
1½ tbs. barbados sugar	2 tbs. double cream

Melt the chocolate in a dessertspoon water. Remove from the heat then gradually add the sugar, egg yolks and cream. Beat the egg whites stiffly and fold them into the mixture. Pour into small glasses and chill well.

219. Lemon Meringue Pie

5 oz. wholewheat flour	*Filling*
2½ oz. margarine	1½ oz. cornflour
2½ oz. lard	½ pint water
water to mix	juice and grated rind of 2
pinch of sea salt	lemons
	2 oz. demerara sugar
Meringue	2 egg yolks
2 egg whites	2 oz. butter
4 oz. demerara sugar	

Make flan case by rubbing the fat into the salted flour and mixing with cold water. Roll out and line flan case. Bake blind for 15 minutes in oven 400 °F. (Reg. 6).

Put water and lemon juice on to boil. Blend cornflour with a little cold water and add to the boiling mixture. Boil for a further 3 minutes then remove from the heat and add 2 oz. sugar, egg yolks and butter. Fill the flan case with this mixture.

Whip up egg whites with the 4 oz. demerara sugar and pile on top. Return to cool oven 300 °F. (Reg. 2) for ½ hour or until the meringue is crisp.

220. Orange Cups

6 oranges	1 oz. powdered gelatine
1 lemon	½ pint boiling water
3 oz. barbados sugar	whipped cream

Squeeze the oranges and the lemon. Dissolve the gelatine and sugar in the water and add to the fruit juices. Pour into the orange halves and decorate with whipped cream when set.

221. Lemon Soufflé

2 lemons	2 dsp. gelatine
2 eggs	5 dsp. water
¼ pint milk	5 dsp. double cream
1½ tbs. barbados sugar	

Bring the milk to the boil and pour on to the egg yolks and sugar. Stir well and cook over gentle heat until thick. Dissolve gelatine in water over low heat, add to egg mixture. Stir in the cream, lemon juice and rind. Beat the egg whites stiffly and fold in.

222. Peach Cream Tarts

2 ripe peaches	5 egg yolks
6 oz. wholewheat flour	½ teasp. vanilla essence
2½ oz. margarine	2 teasp. kirsch
2½ oz. lard	¼ pint double cream
water to mix	
pinch of sea salt	*Syrup*
¼ lb. barbados sugar	2 oz. barbados sugar
3 tbs. cornflour	½ pint water
¾ pint milk	1 vanilla pod or few drops essence

Rub fat into salted wholewheat flour and mix to firm dough with water. Roll out and line four individual pastry cases with mixture. Bake in oven 400 °F. (Reg. 6) for 15 minutes.

Blend the cornflour with a little cold milk. Boil the rest of the milk, add the cornflour mixture and boil for one more minute stirring all the time. Remove from the heat and add the sugar then the beaten egg yolks. Cook in double saucepan for 5 or 10 minutes. Strain and cool. Add vanilla essence and kirsch. Cover and chill well. Half fill the pastry cases.

Heat 2 oz. barbados sugar in ½ pint water, add vanilla pod

or essence and simmer gently for a few minutes. Cut peaches in half and remove the stones; add them to the syrup and cook until tender. Cool and place on top of cream in the pastry cases. Decorate with whipped cream.

223. Syllabub

1 lemon	1 glass white wine (4 oz.)
3 oz. barbados sugar	½ pint double cream

Thinly peel the lemon rind, put it in a basin with the strained juice of the lemon and the wine and leave overnight. Strain the liquid into a deep bowl, stir in the sugar and gradually add the cream. Whisk until the cream is stiff. Serve in long glasses.

224. Raspberry Melon

1 large ripe melon	1 glass white wine
4 oz. barbados sugar	1½ lb. raspberries

Cut the top off the melon and remove all the seeds. Sprinkle the inside with a little of the sugar, pour in the wine and move it around all over the inside of the melon. Chill for 1 hour, then fill with raspberries and sugar in alternate layers. Put the lid of the melon back on and chill for another 2 hours. Serve with a spoon, scooping out melon and raspberries together.

225. Rhubarb Jelly

1 lb. rhubarb	2 oz. cornflour
6 oz. barbados sugar	2 tbs. lemon juice
½ pint water	

Wash and cut up the rhubarb, put in a saucepan with the water and simmer gently until cooked. Remove from heat and add sugar; stir until dissolved. Blend the cornflour with the lemon juice. Strain off the juice from the rhubarb; make up to a pint if necessary. Return the juice to the pan and boil. Add the blended cornflour and boil for a further 5 minutes stirring all the time. Add the rhubarb and pour the mixture into an oiled mould. Turn out when set and serve with cream.

226. Mincemeat Sponge

4 oz. butter
3 oz. barbados sugar
2 eggs
4 oz. wholewheat flour

2 oz. wholewheat bread-
    crumbs
1 lb. mincemeat

Beat butter and sugar together until soft and creamy. Add two beaten eggs then the flour and the breadcrumbs. Add a little milk if mixture is too stiff. Grease a basin and pour in a layer of sponge then a layer of mincemeat and continue until the basin is almost full. Put basin in oven 350 °F. (Reg. 4) for 1 hour. Serve upside-down with cream or custard.

227. Peach Ambrosia

4 peaches
6 oz. barbados sugar
½ pint water
thinly peeled rind of 2 oranges

thinly peeled rind of 2 lemons
juice of 2 lemons
¼ pint whipped cream

Skin the peaches by dipping in boiling water and rubbing with thumb and forefinger. Cut in half, remove the stones and slice. Place in serving dish and sprinkle with lemon juice. Combine sugar, water, orange and lemon rind and boil slowly and carefully for 2 minutes. Pour over peaches and decorate with whipped cream.

228. Strudel Flan

1 oz. barbados sugar	*Filling*
5 oz. wholewheat flour	1 lb. cooking apples
5 oz. butter	1 tbs. barbados sugar
2 oz. unblanched almonds	1 tbs. raisins
1 egg yolk	1 oz. blanched almonds
1 teasp. lemon juice	1 tbs. water
	1 egg white
	1½ oz. demerara sugar

Mix sugar and flour and rub in the fat. Stir in the chopped unblanched almonds and the lemon juice. Bind pastry with lightly beaten egg yolk. Chill dough for ½ hour. Roll out and line oblong pastry tin with mixture and bake blind in oven 400 °F. (Reg. 6) for 20 minutes.

Peel and slice the apples, add sugar, raisins, chopped blanched almonds and water. Simmer gently for 5 minutes, remove from heat and allow to cool. When the pastry case is cool fill with apple mixture.

Whisk up the egg whites with the demerara sugar and pipe in diagonal patterns across the top of the flan. Put in cool oven 300 °F. (Reg. 2–3) for 10 minutes.

229. Rum and Chocolate Mousse

4 oz. sweet cooking chocolate	1 teasp. Nescafé
4 eggs	½ pint double cream
1 teasp. vanilla essence	2 tbs. rum

Melt chocolate in top of double saucepan. Remove from heat and allow to cool. Beat egg yolks lightly and pour gradually into melted chocolate. Add Nescafé dissolved in 1 tbs. hot water and then the vanilla essence. Beat cream until thick and add the rum, then fold into chocolate mixture. Beat egg whites until stiff and then fold into mixture. Pour the mixture into serving bowl and chill for 2 hours.

230. Apple Cake

2¼ lb. cooking apples	4 oz. butter
3 tbs. water	4 oz. wholemeal breadcrumbs
3 oz. barbados sugar	½ lb. marmalade
¼ teasp. ground cinnamon	¼ pint double cream

Peel, slice and cook the apples gently in 3 tbs. water until soft; add half the sugar. Melt the butter in another pan and add the breadcrumbs. Stir for a minute over the heat then add the rest of the sugar. Grease an 8-inch sandwich tin and layer the breadcrumbs, apple and marmalade, sprinkling each marmalade layer with cinnamon. The top layer should be breadcrumbs. Press down firmly and bake in oven 350 °F. (Reg. 4) for ¾ hour. Place the cake on a plate and decorate with whipped cream and marmalade.

231. Pineapple Brulée

12 oz. fresh pineapple	4 oz. demerara sugar
½ pint double cream	

Chop the pineapple into small pieces and put at the bottom of a warm well-buttered dish. Whip the cream fairly stiff and pile it on top of the pineapple. Sprinkle with demerara sugar and put it under the grill until the sugar melts.

232. Ice Box Gateau

3 oz. butter	1 egg
2 oz. barbados sugar	2 oz. grated plain chocolate
½ lb. digestive biscuits	¼ gill rum or brandy or coffee

Cream butter and sugar until light. Add egg yolk and beat again. Crumble the biscuits and moisten them with the chosen liquid. Beat the egg white and fold into butter mixture. Sprinkle half the chocolate on the bottom of a cake tin (7-inch sandwich tin), then add layer of biscuit mixture followed by layer of cream. Top with the rest of the grated chocolate, cover with foil and put cake into refrigerator for 24 hours. Loosen the cake with a palette knife and turn out on to serving dish.

233. **Lemon Wine Jelly**

1 lemon	1 wineglass white wine
1 packet lemon jelly	4 egg yolks
2 oz. barbados sugar	2 egg whites

Peel the lemon thinly. Cover rind with a little water and simmer for about 10 minutes. Strain into a pint jug, add the juice of the lemon, the lemon jelly and the sugar. Add the wine and make up to a pint with boiling water. Stir until the jelly has dissolved. Beat the egg yolks and the two whites together and add to the mixture. Place the basin in a saucepan of water and heat, stirring all the time until the mixture thickens. Pour into an oiled mould and when set turn out and serve with whipped cream.

234. **Raspberry Brulée**

1 lb. fresh raspberries	½ pint double cream
or	2 oz. demerara sugar
2 packets frozen raspberries	

Fill dish with layers of raspberries and whipped cream, ending with cream. Sprinkle with demerara sugar and put under hot grill to brown and crisp the sugar.

235. **Apple Flan**

8 oz. minced apple	*Pastry*
2 eggs	4 oz. wholewheat flour
4 oz. butter	pinch sea salt
3 oz. barbados sugar	1½ oz. margarine
	1½ oz. lard
	water

Make pastry case by rubbing fat into salted wholewheat flour and mixing with a little water. Roll out, line flan tin and bake blind for 15 minutes in oven 375 °F. (Reg. 5).

Cream butter and sugar, stir in minced apple and two well-beaten eggs. When pastry case is cool fill with this mixture. Serve with whipped cream.

236. Butterscotch Meringue Flan

Pastry

4 oz. wholewheat flour
pinch sea salt
1½ oz. lard
1½ oz. margarine
water

Filling

2 oz. butter

4 oz. barbados sugar
1 egg
2 oz. demerara sugar
1 oz. cornflour
¼ teasp. sea salt
8 oz. milk
2 tbs. water

Rub the fat into the salted flour and mix to a dough with cold water. Roll out and line a 7-inch sandwich tin. Bake blind for 15 minutes in oven 375 °F. (Reg. 5).

Melt the butter and barbados sugar together in a double saucepan, add the beaten egg yolk then the cornflour blended with cold water, finally milk and a pinch of sea salt. Cook the mixture until it thickens. Allow to cool a little then pour into flan case. Whip up the egg white with 2 oz. demerara sugar and pile on top. Return to cool oven for ½ hour or until meringue is crisp.

237. Pineapple Surprise

1 small pineapple
½ lb. marshmallows
juice of 1 lemon

½ pint double cream
2 oz. barbados sugar

Shred the pineapple into small pieces and mix with the chopped up marshmallows. Chill in the refrigerator for 1 hour. Pour the juice of the lemon over the mixture. Whip up the cream with the sugar and fold into the mixture, pour into serving dish.

238. Banana Surprise

6 bananas	2 egg whites
2 oz. barbados sugar	¼ pint double cream
1 orange	

Mash the bananas with the sugar, then add the rind and juice of the orange; beat well until light and frothy. Beat the egg whites until stiff and fold into the mixture. Serve with whipped cream.

239. Lemon Cheese

2 eggs	½ tbs. gelatine
3 oz. barbados sugar	2 tbs. water
1 lemon	½ pint whipped cream

Beat the egg yolks and the sugar until light and fluffy, add the rind and juice of the lemon. Dissolve the gelatine in 2 tbs. hot water and add to the egg mixture, stirring continually until thickened. Beat the two egg whites very stiffly and fold into the mixture. Fold in the whipped cream and pour into an oiled mould. Chill for 3 hours.

240. Apple Sundae

2 eating apples	2 oz. chopped nuts
1½ oz. barbados sugar	4 maraschino cherries
½ pint yoghourt	

Wash the unpeeled apples and shred coarsely. Put into individual glasses, sprinkle on the sugar and add alternate layers of chopped nuts and yoghourt. Decorate with a cherry.

241. Apple and Mincemeat Crunch

8 oz. mincemeat
8 oz. sieved cooked apple
1 tbs. brandy
8 oz. self-raising wholewheat
  flour

4 oz. butter
5 oz. barbados sugar
grated peel of 1 lemon

Mix the apple, mincemeat and brandy and put into an oven-proof dish. Rub the butter into the flour, add the sugar and lemon peel and put into the refrigerator for a few hours. Put the crumble on top of the apple mixture and bake in oven 425 °F. (Reg. 7) for 40 minutes.

242. Chocolate Pudding

2½ oz. chocolate
2½ oz. butter
2½ oz. barbados sugar
2½ oz. ground almonds
4 eggs

Sauce
3 oz. barbados sugar
4 oz. plain chocolate
¼ pint water

Grease a pudding basin and sprinkle lightly with barbados sugar. Cream butter and sugar and add the egg yolks one by one. Whip egg whites stiffly and fold into the mixture. Add ground almonds and grated chocolate. Pour into the basin, cover with foil and steam for ¾ hour. To make the sauce put the sugar, ¼ pint water and the chocolate into a double sauce-pan and cook gently until thick. Turn the pudding on to the serving dish and pour the sauce over the top. Serve with whipped cream.

243. Dorset Apple Cake

4 oz. self-raising wholewheat
  flour
pinch sea salt
3 oz. barbados sugar

2 oz. butter
2 eggs
1 lb. apples

Cream the butter and sugar together, add the beaten eggs then the salted flour. Stir in the apples, peeled, cored and chopped up finely. Turn mixture into greased fireproof dish and bake in oven 375 °F. (Reg. 5) for 45 minutes. Serve with soft brown sugar and cream.

244. Apricot Rice

½ lb. stewed dried apricots	3 oz. barbados sugar
2 oz. natural brown rice	1 pint milk
3 eggs	nut of butter

Put apricots at the bottom of a greased fireproof dish. Add the rice. Whisk the milk, sugar and eggs together and pour over the rice. Dot with butter and bake in oven 350 °F. (Reg. 4) for 1½ hours.

245. Caramel Oranges

6 oranges	4 tbs. toasted slivered almonds
8 oz. barbados sugar	whipped cream
2 oz. butter	2 oz. water

Dissolve the sugar in the water over a low heat stirring all the time until the syrup is dark brown. Remove from heat; add the butter and stir until smooth. Peel the oranges removing all the white skin. Slice thinly and arrange on a serving dish in overlapping layers. Pour the sauce over the oranges and sprinkle with almonds. Serve with whipped cream.

246. Date and Apple Torte

¾ lb. sliced cooking apples	½ teasp. powdered mace
2 oz. chopped walnuts	6 oz. self-raising wholewheat
4 oz. chopped dates	flour
4 oz. butter	2 beaten eggs
3 oz. barbados sugar	1 tbs. brandy or cider

Cream butter and sugar together then add the powdered mace,

flour and the beaten eggs. Stir in the apples, dates and chopped walnuts, then 1 tbs. of brandy or cider. Turn into well-buttered pie-dish and cook in oven 350 °F. (Reg. 4) for 40 minutes. Serve with whipped cream.

247. Peach Pastries

4 fresh peaches	1½ oz. barbados sugar
3 oz. hazel nuts, toasted and ground	4 oz. wholewheat flour
	pinch of sea salt
3 oz. butter	½ pint double cream

Work the butter into the sugar, salted flour and ground nuts until paste is formed. Chill for ½ hour. Divide into three and roll out. Bake in moderate oven 350 °F. (Reg. 4) for 15 minutes. Cool, then sandwich together the layers with whipped cream and sliced peaches.

8-Savouries or Supper Dishes

248. Cheese Soufflé
249. Cheese Potato Fritters
250. Cheese Balls
251. Cheese, Tomato and Cauliflower Mould
252. Cream Cheese and Tomato Fritters
253. Cheese Pops
254. Cheese Fondue
255. Cheese Flan
256. Cheese Tomato Pie
257. Stuffed Potatoes
258. Cheese, Ham and Chicory Pie
259. Cream Cheese Gateau
260. Cheese Potato Pie
261. Beefburghers
262. Stuffed Cabbage Rolls
263. Savoury Meat Balls
264. Dutch Meat Balls
265. Baked Lasagne
266. Spaghetti Carbonara
267. Spaghetti Bolognese
268. Chinese Pancakes
269. Chinese Fried Rice
270. Risotto
271. Pilav
272. Paella
273. Stuffed Rolls
274. Lentil Cakes
275. Chupatties
276. Cauliflower Fritters
277. Mushroom Pancakes
278. Savoury Mushrooms
279. Mushroom Scallops
280. Stuffed Mushrooms
281. Pizza
282. Quiche Lorraine
283. Ham and Pineapple Flan
284. Tomato Jelly
285. Corn Scramble
286. Devilled Potato Salad
287. Stuffed Eggs
288. Spanish Omelette
289. Devilled Eggs
290. Chinese Egg Casserole
291. Jellied Eggs
292. Egg, Tomato and Potato Pie
293. Irish Omelette

248. Cheese Soufflé

3 oz. butter	3 egg yolks
1 oz. wholewheat flour	4 egg whites
½ pint warm milk	4 oz. grated cheddar cheese
a sprinkle of parmesan cheese	sea salt and pepper

Melt butter in thick pan; add flour gradually and mix to a smooth paste stirring all the time; then add the warm milk slowly, and cook until sauce is thick and creamy. Remove from the heat and add the egg yolks beaten to a pale yellow consistency; add the cheese, season well and return to the heat until the cheese has melted but do not boil. Whisk the egg whites until they are stiff and fold them into the cheese mixture. Pile mixture into a buttered soufflé dish, sprinkle with parmesan and cook for 40 minutes in oven 400 °F. (Reg. 6).

249. Cheese Potato Fritters

2 onions	4 oz. grated cheddar cheese
2 oz. butter	sea salt and pepper
4 sliced cooked potatoes	4 eggs

Slice onions finely and fry gently in the butter until they are soft. Add the sliced potatoes and the cheese to the pan with plenty of sea salt and pepper and fry until golden brown. Turn the fritter over and let it brown on the other side. Place gently on to serving dish, fry four eggs and place on top.

250. Cheese Balls

2 oz. grated cheddar cheese	sea salt, pepper and cayenne
1 oz. wholewheat flour	vegetable oil for frying
2 eggs	

Mix cheese and flour. Beat up the egg yolks, season well and add to cheese mixture. Whip the egg whites until stiff and fold into the mixture. Drop the mixture by teaspoonfuls into the hot oil and deep fry until golden brown. Place on greaseproof paper and serve very hot.

251. Cheese, Tomato and Cauliflower Mould

1 cooked cauliflower	½ pint tomato juice
3 oz. grated cheddar cheese	1 oz. gelatine
½ pint milk	sea salt and pepper
1 oz. wholewheat flour	1 teasp. barbados sugar
1 oz. butter	1 tbs. chopped parsley

Make white sauce by melting butter in pan, adding the flour then gradually stirring in the warmed milk. Boil and season well. Break the cauliflower into small sprigs and add to the sauce. Stir in most of the cheese and allow to cool. Dissolve the gelatine in the tomato juice, add the sugar and season well. Mix the tomato juice into the cauliflower mixture and when nearly setting pour into oiled mould. When set turn out and serve sprinkled with cheese and chopped parsley.

252. Cream Cheese and Tomato Fritters

4 slices wholewheat bread	egg and wholewheat bread-
2 oz. cream cheese	crumbs for coating
sea salt and pepper	vegetable oil for deep frying
2 tomatoes	

Cut the crusts off the bread slices and spread each slice with cream cheese. Sprinkle with sea salt and pepper and top with thin slices of tomato. Sandwich slices together in twos, dip in beaten egg, coat with wholewheat breadcrumbs and fry in deep oil until crisp and golden.

253. Cheese Pops

½ oz. wholewheat flour	½ pint milk
4 teasp. sea salt	2 oz. grated cheddar cheese
2 eggs	

Put flour seasoned with sea salt into bowl. Beat up eggs with milk and add to flour mixture. Beat well for 5 minutes and leave to stand for 1 hour. Oil or grease some patty tins, heat. Add grated cheese to batter and half fill the patty tins with mixture. Bake in hot oven 450 °F. (Reg. 8) for 15–20 minutes or until crisp and brown. Eat at once spread with butter.

254. Cheese Fondue

4 oz. diced gruyère cheese
1 clove garlic
1 wineglass white wine
1 teasp. cornflour

1 wineglass kirsch
sea salt, pepper, dash of nutmeg

Place diced cheese in earthenware casserole which has first been rubbed well with garlic, cover with white wine and cook over hot flame stirring constantly. When the cheese has melted allow to cool for a few minutes. Pour kirsch on cornflour, mix well and add to cheese mixture. Season well.

Place casserole over spirit flame in the middle of the table, put crusty pieces of wholewheat bread on the ends of forks and dip into the cheese mixture.

255. Cheese Flan

Pastry
6 oz. wholewheat flour
1 teasp. sea salt
2½ oz. margarine
2½ oz. lard
water to bind

Filling
1½ lb. sliced onions

2 tbs. vegetable oil
1 oz. butter
1 egg
2 tbs. cream
sea salt, pepper
sprinkle of nutmeg
4 oz. grated cheese

Cut margarine and lard into seasoned flour and bind with a little water. Roll out and line 8-inch flan tin or ring. Bake blind in oven 400 °F. (Reg. 6) for 15 minutes.

Sauté onions gently in the butter and oil. Beat eggs, cream

and seasonings with 1 oz. grated cheese, add onions and pour into flan ring. Sprinkle with the rest of the cheese and turn to a moderate oven 350 °F. (Reg. 4) for 30 minutes.

256. Cheese Tomato Pie

1 lb. tomatoes	4 oz. grated cheddar cheese
4 oz. wholewheat bread- crumbs	sea salt and pepper
	1 oz. butter

Dip tomatoes in boiling water and peel. Slice tomatoes and arrange a layer in the bottom of a pie-dish. Cover with a layer of wholewheat breadcrumbs and then a layer of grated cheese. Continue thus, seasoning each layer and finishing with a layer of grated cheese. Dot with butter and bake in oven 350 °F. (Reg. 4) until top is crisp and golden.

257. Stuffed Potatoes

4 large potatoes	4 oz. grated cheddar cheese
1 oz. butter	sea salt and pepper
¼ pint milk	8 eggs

Bake the potatoes in their jackets, cut them in half lengthwise and scoop out the inside. Mash this with the butter and the milk and season well. Mix in the grated cheese and fill the jackets with this mixture. Make a little hollow in the middle of each potato and break an egg into each hollow, sprinkle with cheese and return to the oven until the egg whites have set.

258. Cheese, Ham and Chicory Pie

8 heads of chicory	½ pint milk
8 thin slices ham	sea salt and pepper
2 oz. butter	4 oz. grated cheddar cheese
1½ oz. wholewheat flour	pinch of nutmeg

Cook chicory by simmering gently in salted water until it is tender. Drain well then wrap each head in a thin slice of ham and place in the bottom of a pie-dish. Melt butter in a pan, add the wholewheat flour and stir for a few minutes then add the warmed milk and boil until thick and creamy. Add the grated cheese and the seasonings. Pour sauce over the chicory and ham, sprinkle with grated cheese and dots of butter. Place under the grill to brown.

259. Cream Cheese Gateau

6 oz. wholewheat flour	6 oz. cream cheese
2½ oz. margarine	¼ pint double cream
2½ oz. lard	2 sliced peaches
2 tbs. single cream	walnut halves and black
sea salt	grapes to garnish

Rub the fat into the salted wholewheat flour and bind with single cream. Wrap in foil and allow to stand in a cool place for 1 hour. Roll out the dough and line a 7-inch flan ring. Prick base and bake blind in fairly hot oven 400 °F. (Reg. 6) for 20 minutes. Turn out on to a wire rack and allow to cool.

Beat the cheese until soft and then stir in the double cream. Place the sliced peaches in the base of the flan ring and pile the cream cheese mixture on the top. Decorate the gateau with nuts and grapes.

260. Cheese Potato Pie

1 lb. sliced cooked potatoes	1 oz. wholewheat flour
4 oz. grated cheddar cheese	1 oz. butter
½ pint milk	sea salt and pepper
1 sliced onion	1 tbs. chopped parsley

Melt butter in heavy pan, stir in the flour and gradually add the warm milk. Stir until thick and creamy, season well, remove from the heat and stir in most of the grated cheese. Place sliced potatoes in pie-dish, sprinkle with sliced onion and chopped parsley and pour over the cheese sauce. Sprinkle with the rest of the grated cheese and place under the grill until crisp and brown.

261. Beefburghers

1 lb. raw minced beef
1 teasp. Marmite
1 minced onion
1 minced clove garlic
mixed herbs

sea salt and pepper
tomato sauce
a little stock
baps and fried onions to serve

Mix meat and onion and flavour with a little Marmite or beef extract, the garlic and some mixed herbs. Form into flat patties but do not compress the meat too much. Cook for a few minutes in an ungreased heavy pan then turn over and cook on the other side; season well and remove from the pan. Stir a little stock into the pan juices and a little tomato sauce. Place the beefburghers in a split bap, sprinkle with sauce and a few crisply fried onions and serve.

262. Stuffed Cabbage Rolls

8 large cabbage leaves
½ lb. minced beef
½ lb. minced pork
1 minced onion
1 tbs. apple cider vinegar
2 oz. butter

1 tbs. chopped parsley
½ teasp. sea salt
½ teasp. thyme
½ mashed clove of garlic
1½ tbs. barbados sugar
½ pint tomato sauce

Wash the cabbage leaves, put into cold water, bring to the boil and cook for 1 minute. Drain, put the leaves into cold water and drain again. Combine the beef, pork, parsley, onion, sea salt, thyme and garlic. Add vinegar and the barbados sugar and mix well. Divide into 8 portions, place one on each cabbage leaf, form into parcels and secure with cotton. Put the parcels in a baking dish, dot with butter, cover with thick tomato sauce and bake in oven 350 °F. (Reg. 4) for 1 hour.

263. Savoury Meat Balls

12 oz. minced beef
4 oz. minced pork
½ pint milk
1 teasp. sea salt
pinch of pepper, allspice,
  powdered cloves

2 oz. wholewheat bread-
  crumbs
1 sliced onion
4 oz. butter
1 egg

Mix beef and pork together and blend with the milk, breadcrumbs, onion, sea salt, pepper, allspice and cloves. Shape the
mixture into small balls and dip in beaten egg. Fry them in
butter, remove them on to the serving dish and pour over them
the meat juices from the pan.

264. Dutch Meat Balls

1 lb. minced beef
1 oz. butter
1½ oz. wholewheat flour
½ pint beef broth
sea salt, pepper, pinch nutmeg

1 tbs. Maggi sauce
egg and wholewheat bread-
  crumbs for coating
vegetable oil for deep frying

Simmer mince until cooked, strain. Melt the butter in a pan,
stir in the flour and cook for a few minutes stirring all the
time. Remove from heat and allow to cool. Boil the broth and
add to the butter and flour; boil, then stir in the meat, and the
seasonings; mix well and allow to cool for several hours. When
cold make the balls and coat with egg and wholewheat breadcrumbs. Deep fry in vegetable oil, drain and serve.

265. Baked Lasagne

1 lb. minced beef	*Cheese mixture*
1 tbs. vegetable oil	12 oz. cottage cheese
1 minced clove garlic	1 beaten egg
1 tbs. chopped parsley	1 teasp. sea salt, pepper
1 tbs. chopped basil	1 tbs. chopped parsley
2 teasp. sea salt	2 oz. parmesan cheese
1 lb. tomatoes	8 oz. Edam or any soft cheese,
6 oz. tomato paste	sliced thinly
	1 lb. lasagne noodles

Brown mince in oil in heavy pan. Add garlic, herbs, seasoning, peeled chopped tomatoes, and tomato paste. Simmer uncovered for 1 hour until thick, stirring occasionally.

Boil lasagne noodles carefully in boiling salted water for 20 minutes, drain and rinse with cold water.

Make cheese mixture by blending cottage cheese with beaten egg and adding the parmesan cheese, parsley and seasonings. Place noodles at the bottom of a greased pie-dish, then layers of cheese mixture, cheese slices and meat mixture and continue in layers until the dish is full, ending with meat mixture and a sprinkle of parmesan cheese. Place in oven 350 °F. (Reg. 4) for ¾ hour.

266. Spaghetti Carbonara

1 lb. long spaghetti	1 oz. butter
6 rashers of streaky bacon	5 beaten eggs

Cook spaghetti in boiling salted water for 20 minutes. Dice the rashers of bacon and fry until crisp. Drain and rinse spaghetti. Return to pan and add melted butter and 5 beaten eggs. Shake the pan and stir the spaghetti so that it is well covered with egg. Add the bacon, mix well and serve with parmesan cheese.

267. Spaghetti Bolognese

8 oz. long spaghetti	1 shredded carrot
1 oz. butter	½ lb. minced raw beef
1 tbs. olive oil	4 oz. tomato purée
2 crushed cloves of garlic	1 bay leaf
2 oz. sliced mushrooms	¾ pint stock
1 chopped onion	sea salt and pepper

Heat butter and oil in a heavy pan and fry garlic, mushrooms, onion and carrot. Stir in the minced beef and fry for several minutes. Add the rest of the ingredients, bring to the boil stirring all the time. Cover and simmer for ½ hour until thick and rich. Boil spaghetti in salted water for 20 minutes. Drain and rinse in cold water. Put spaghetti on large serving dish and pour over the bolognese sauce. Serve with parmesan cheese.

268. Chinese Pancakes

1 lb. diced cooked pork	4 oz. wholewheat flour
½ lb. cooked shrimps	1 egg
1 carrot	sea salt
1 stick celery	¼ pint milk
1 teasp. soya sauce	¼ pint water
sea salt, pepper	4 oz. lard
1 teasp. chopped chives	deep fat for frying
1 teasp. barbados sugar	

Shred the carrot and the celery and mix with the chopped chives, pork, shrimps and seasoning. Add the soya sauce.

Make the batter by beating salted flour with the egg, milk and water. Melt a little lard in a heavy pan, pour in some batter and cook the pancake on one side only. Turn and spread the pork filling on the uncooked side and roll up quickly. Seal the ends with some uncooked batter. When all the pancakes have been prepared in this way drop them one by one into boiling fat and cook until golden brown.

269. Chinese Fried Rice

4 oz. olive oil
5 eggs beaten with salt
sea salt
2 tbs. sherry
1 tbs. soya sauce
4 tbs. stock
¼ lb. cooked shrimps

¼ lb. diced cooked chicken
¼ lb. cooked ham or pork diced
4 oz. sliced mushrooms
¼ lb. cooked green peas
8 oz. natural brown rice

Boil the rice in salted water for 20 minutes, drain and dry. Heat 2 tbs. olive oil and lightly fry half the beaten eggs. Cut into strips and keep warm. Heat a further 2 tbs. oil and gently fry the shrimps. Reduce the heat and add the chicken, ham, mushrooms and peas. Heat through and keep on one side. Heat the rest of the oil, add rice and stir constantly over a low heat. Add stock, sherry, soya sauce and season to taste. Mix all the ingredients together and add the rest of the beaten eggs. Heat through and serve.

270. Risotto

8 oz. natural brown rice
1 chopped onion
3 oz. butter
1½ pints chicken stock (more if necessary)
4 oz. chopped parsley
2 oz. parmesan cheese

4 oz. dry white wine
2 oz. raisins
4 diced chicken livers
4 oz. diced cooked ham or pork
sea salt and pepper

Fry onion gently in the butter in a thick pan. Do not brown. Add the rice and fry for a few minutes stirring constantly. Reduce the wine to 2 oz. by heating quickly and add it to the rice. Add the raisins, stock and seasoning. Cover with tight-fitting lid, lower heat and cook for 15 minutes or until the rice is tender. Add chicken livers and ham and cook for a further few minutes over low heat. Stir in the parsley and the parmesan cheese.

271. Pilav

1 lb. lean lamb diced
2 oz. butter
¾ pint stock
8 oz. natural brown rice
1 sliced onion

1 chopped stick of celery
1 chopped clove of garlic
sea salt, pepper, pinch
   cayenne

Boil butter and stock, add the rice and boil rapidly for 5 minutes. Lower heat, cover with a lid and continue to cook until all the liquid is absorbed and the rice is cooked. Fry the meat then add the onion, celery, garlic, sea salt and pepper to taste. Stir the meat mixture into the rice and serve piping hot. A rich tomato sauce may be served with it.

272. Paella

1 lb. natural brown rice
8 oz. olive oil
1 sliced onion
½ lb. peeled and sliced tomatoes
2 oz. sliced green olives
8 oz. diced cooked chicken

4 oz. cooked prawns
1 sliced green pepper
4 oz. cooked green peas
2 pints stock
sea salt and pepper
pinch of saffron

Heat the oil in a large heavy pan and fry the onion, tomatoes, chicken, prawns, green pepper, olives and peas. Cook gently for 10 minutes, season well then add the rice. Cook for a further 5 minutes stirring all the time. Add 2 pints boiling stock and continue cooking the entire mixture for about 20 minutes until the rice is soft and the liquid absorbed. Add a pinch of saffron dissolved in 1 tbs. of hot water. Serve paella in the pan it has been cooked in.

273. Stuffed Rolls

4 wholemeal rolls
2 oz. grated cheddar cheese
2 peeled and sliced tomatoes

4 dsp. chutney
sea salt and pepper

Run cold water over the rolls, pat gently and dry. Split, spread with butter and fill with cheese, tomatoes and chutney and season with sea salt and pepper. Put rolls on baking tray in hot oven 400 °F. (Reg. 6) for 12 minutes. Serve with watercress.

274. Lentil Cakes

4 oz. lentils
½ pint water
1 dsp. dripping
1 chopped onion
1 teasp. tomato paste
pinch thyme, mace, sea salt
  and pepper

2 tbs. ground rice
1 egg
4 oz. wholewheat bread-
  crumbs
deep oil for frying

Wash and soak lentils overnight. Drain and put in the pan with water, dripping, onion, tomato paste, herbs and seasoning. Cover pan and simmer mixture gently for 2 hours. Add ground rice and cook for 10 minutes or until the mixture is stiff, stirring constantly. Form into four flat cakes, egg and breadcrumb and fry in deep oil.

275. Chupatties

½ lb. wholewheat flour
1 oz. butter

cold water
sea salt

Rub the butter into the flour, add salt and enough cold water to make a soft dough. Cover and leave for 1 hour or longer. Knead well and divide into small balls and roll each one out to the size of a tea plate. Cook them over slow heat on a greased griddle, turning over several times.

276. Cauliflower Fritters

1 cauliflower	2 oz. wholewheat flour
3 oz. olive oil	$\frac{1}{8}$ pint water
2 oz. apple cider vinegar	1 dsp. vegetable oil
pinch of powdered garlic	1 egg white
$\frac{1}{2}$ teasp. barbados sugar	deep fat or oil for frying
sea salt and pepper	grated cheddar cheese to serve

Wash the cauliflower and break into small sprigs. Cook them in boiling salted water for 10 minutes until almost cooked. Drain, turn into a bowl and leave to soak for 1 hour in french dressing made by mixing the olive oil, apple cider vinegar, garlic, sea salt, pepper and barbados sugar.

Make batter by beating together the flour, water, vegetable oil and then incorporating the whipped egg white. Drain the cauliflower sprigs again, dip in batter mixture and fry in deep oil until crisp and golden. Serve sprinkled with grated cheese.

277. Mushroom Pancakes

$\frac{1}{2}$ lb. wholewheat flour	*Filling*
sea salt	$\frac{1}{2}$ lb. sliced mushrooms
2 large eggs	1 minced onion
$\frac{1}{2}$ pint milk	1 dsp. chopped parsley
2 tbs. water	1 beaten egg
2 oz. grated cheese	1 oz. grated cheese
4 oz. butter	sea salt and pepper

Make the pancake batter by beating together the salted flour with the eggs, milk and water for 10 minutes. Leave to stand for 1 hour if possible then add 2 oz. grated cheese.

Make the filling by frying the mushrooms in a little butter then adding the onion, parsley, sea salt and pepper and finally the beaten egg and grated cheese and continue to cook until the egg is set and holding the ingredients together.

Melt a knob of butter in the pan and when really hot pour in some batter. Cook gently on both sides. Spread the pancake with the filling, fold and keep warm. Repeat until all the batter and filling have been used up.

278. Savoury Mushrooms

8 large mushrooms
4 oz. cottage cheese
1 teasp. apple cider vinegar
1 teasp. barbados sugar

2 teasp. vegetable oil
1 teasp. tomato purée or paste
sea salt and pepper
4 slices wholemeal toast

Mix the oil, vinegar, tomato purée, sugar and seasoning. Heat mixture in pan and gently cook the mushroom caps in this mixture. Remove caps, drain and keep warm. When the liquid in the pan is cold blend in the cottage cheese. Pile cheese mixture into mushroom caps and serve on hot wholemeal buttered toast.

279. Mushroom Scallops

½ lb. sliced mushrooms
2 oz. butter
sea salt, pepper, cayenne
4 oz. wholewheat bread-
crumbs

pinch powdered nutmeg
1 beaten egg
1 tbs. double cream

Cook the sliced mushrooms gently in the butter, season well then stir in the breadcrumbs and nutmeg. Add the beaten egg and the double cream. Put mixture into scallop shells, top with breadcrumbs and dot with butter. Put under the grill for a few minutes to brown.

280. Stuffed Mushrooms

1 lb. mushrooms
3 oz. butter
2 tbs. wholemeal bread-
crumbs
1 tbs. minced meat
1 tbs. grated cheese

1 teasp. chopped parsley
a little stock
sea salt and pepper
pinch nutmeg
4 slices wholemeal toast

Take 8 large mushrooms and remove stalks. Chop the remaining mushrooms and the 8 stalks and mix with breadcrumbs, minced meat, cheese, parsley, seasoning and stock and fry gently in the butter for a few minutes. Put in the pinch of nutmeg and pile the mixture into the mushroom caps. Bake in oven 350 °F. (Reg. 4) for 15 minutes and serve on hot buttered wholemeal toast.

281. Pizza

1 lb. wholewheat flour
2 teasp. sea salt
1 tbs. olive oil
¼ pint water
½ oz. fresh yeast (or 2 teasp. dried yeast)
1 teasp. barbados sugar
¼ pint water

Topping
Anchovy fillets
capers
black olives
onion rings

Filling
1 lb. grated cheddar cheese
1 lb. sliced tomatoes
1 teasp. basil or thyme
pepper

Mix flour and salt in bowl. Dissolve the yeast and sugar in warm water and let it stand for 10 minutes then add it to the flour with the oil and enough water to make a soft dough. Knead dough for about 5 minutes on lightly floured board. Shape the dough into a large ball, put it in a bowl, cover with a lid and leave it in a warm place to rise and double in size. Turn out and knead lightly, shaping it into a long strip. Brush with oil and roll up. Repeat this three times. Divide the dough into 6 pieces and roll each piece into a flat circle to fit greased sponge tins. Brush the dough with oil and cover with alternate layers of grated cheese and sliced tomatoes sprinkled with herbs and pepper, ending with a layer of cheese. Decorate with anchovy fillets, capers and black olives. Add onion rings before or after baking. Bake in oven 450 °F. (Reg. 8) for 15–20 minutes.

282. Quiche Lorraine

¼ lb. wholewheat flour	4 slices streaky bacon
1½ oz. lard	2 sliced tomatoes
1½ oz. margarine	1 chopped onion
1 teasp. sea salt	4 oz. grated cheddar cheese
a little water	2 beaten eggs
1 tbs. chopped parsley	sea salt and pepper

Make shortcrust pastry by rubbing fat into salted flour and adding enough water to make a soft dough. Roll out and line a flan case with the dough. Fry bacon until crisp then chop and spread over flan case. Cover with sliced tomatoes and the chopped onion. Pour over the beaten eggs seasoned with sea salt and pepper and top with a good layer of grated cheese. Sprinkle with parsley and bake in oven 400 °F. (Reg. 6) for 30 minutes.

283. Ham and Pineapple Flan

¼ lb. wholewheat flour	½ oz. butter
1½ oz. lard	½ oz. wholewheat flour
1½ oz. margarine	¼ pint milk
1 teasp. sea salt	sea salt and pepper
a little water	1 egg yolk
¼ lb. sliced cooked ham	2 oz. grated cheddar cheese
4 oz. diced fresh pineapple	

Make flan case by rubbing fat into salted flour and adding enough water to make a soft dough. Roll out and line the flan ring. Spread ham over the bottom of the case and cover with a layer of pineapple. Melt a little butter in a pan, stir in the flour and gradually add the milk. Cook until smooth and creamy stirring all the time. Add the egg yolk and mix in most of the grated cheese with a little sea salt and pepper. Pour sauce over pineapple and ham, sprinkle with grated cheese and bake in oven 400 °F. (Reg. 6) for 30 minutes.

284. Tomato Jelly

1 pint tomato soup
½ oz. powdered gelatine

1 tbs. grated onion
1 teasp. barbados sugar

Heat tomato soup and sprinkle in the gelatine, stir until well dissolved. Stir in grated onion and sugar. Pour into wetted ring mould and leave to set. Turn out when cold and fill the centre with vegetable salad.

285. Corn Scramble

1 small tin of whole kernel sweet corn
1 oz. butter
2 large eggs

1 tbs. milk
sea salt and pepper
slices of wholemeal toast

Drain sweet corn and heat gently. Melt butter in a pan, add beaten eggs and milk and stir until mixture thickens. Add corn, mix well and serve on hot buttered toast.

286. Devilled Potato Salad

2 lb. new potatoes
1 tbs. apple cider vinegar
sea salt and pepper
3 apples
3 sticks sliced celery
3 slices streaky bacon chopped up and cooked crisply

½ pint sour cream
¼ pint mayonnaise (see page 11)
pinch of curry powder
squeeze of lemon juice
1 tbs. chopped parsley

Boil the new potatoes in their skins until just tender. Drain, peel and slice. Toss in cider vinegar, season with sea salt and pepper and allow to cool. Add diced apples, celery and bacon. Blend sour cream, mayonnaise, curry powder and lemon juice and toss potato mixture in this sauce. Sprinkle with chopped parsley and serve.

287. Stuffed Eggs

4 hard-boiled eggs cut lengthwise
6 tbs. mayonnaise (see page
11)
1 tbs. apple cider vinegar

½ teasp. french mustard
sea salt and pepper
1 tbs. chopped parsley
slices of wholemeal toast

Remove the egg yolks and mash with mayonnaise, mustard, sea salt and pepper and vinegar. Refill egg whites, sprinkle with chopped parsley and serve on slices of wholemeal buttered toast.

288. Spanish Omelette

1 cooked potato
1 onion
2 tomatoes
2 tbs. olive oil
pinch of cayenne pepper

1 tbs. apple cider vinegar
4 eggs
4 teasp. water
sea salt and pepper

Peel and slice the potato, slice the onion and the tomatoes and cook slowly in half the oil until soft. Season well and sprinkle with apple cider vinegar. Beat the eggs lightly in a bowl, add the water and the sea salt and pepper. Add the potato mixture and pour into a hot omelette pan with the rest of the oil. Turn the omelette when it is brown on one side. Serve hot in slices with a green salad.

289. Devilled Eggs

1 lb. spinach
4 hard-boiled eggs
1 oz. butter
1 teasp. curry powder
1 oz. wholewheat flour

½ pint milk
1 teasp. mustard
¼ teasp. sea salt
pinch of cayenne
few drops apple cider vinegar

Wash the spinach well and cook in a little boiling salted water. Drain and chop very finely. Put in the bottom of a dish and

147

slice the eggs on top of it. Melt the butter, stir in the flour,
mustard, curry powder and seasoning and gradually add the
milk. Lastly add the vinegar but do not boil. Coat eggs with
sauce and reheat for 10 minutes.

290. Chinese Egg Casserole

1 lb. minced chicken or beef   1 teacup water
10 eggs   corn oil
1 chicken bouillon cube   sea salt and pepper

Season the mince well, fry lightly in corn oil and place in
bottom of a shallow casserole dish. Make bouillon by dissolv-
ing the cube in hot water. Allow to cool until quite cold. Pour
the cold bouillon over the mince. Beat the eggs and season
well with sea salt and pepper. Pour eggs into the bouillon.
Cook in oven 325 °F. (Reg. 3) until top has set and looks like
a custard, about ½ hour.

291. Jellied Eggs

4 eggs   ½ pint water
2 oz. cooked ham   ¼ oz. powdered gelatine
a few tarragon leaves   1 tbs. apple cider vinegar
½ a chicken bouillon cube

Poach the eggs in gently simmering water to which has been
added 1 tbs. apple cider vinegar. Line small individual dishes
with strips of ham. When the eggs are cooked, drained and
cold, put one into each dish. Decorate with tarragon leaves.
Dissolve the chicken bouillon cube in hot water and stir in the
gelatine. When almost set pour over the eggs and leave to set.

292. Egg, Tomato and Potato Pie

4 eggs
4 oz. seasoned wholewheat breadcrumbs
½ lb. tomatoes
sea salt and pepper

pinch of barbados sugar
1 lb. cooked mashed potatoes
2 oz. butter
2 oz. grated cheddar cheese

Line a greased ovenproof dish with breadcrumbs. Place a layer of peeled and sliced tomatoes at the bottom and sprinkle with sea salt and pepper and a pinch of barbados sugar. Cover with a layer of mashed potatoes. Beat up the four eggs and pour over the mashed potatoes. Sprinkle with breadcrumbs then a layer of sliced tomatoes and finely another layer of mashed potatoes. Sprinkle with grated cheddar cheese and bake in oven 350 °F. (Reg. 4) for ½ hour.

293. Irish Omelette

4 oz. streaky bacon
1 chopped onion
1 cooked diced potato
pinch of mixed herbs

1 oz. butter
sea salt and pepper
4 beaten eggs

Cut bacon into small pieces and fry with onion, potato, butter, herbs and seasoning. Stir in beaten eggs and cook gently until eggs are set.

9-Sandwich Fillings and Party Snacks

Sandwich Fillings

294. Cream Cheese and Red Pepper
295. Sardine Spread
296. Nut and Raisin
297. Cream Cheese and Watercress
298. Cream Cheese and Chutney
299. Sardine and Tomato
300. Liver Pâté and Cucumber
301. Ham, Eggs and Chives
302. Honey and Nuts
303. Marmite and Watercress
304. Bacon
305. Cheese and Celery
306. Curried Egg
307. Banana and Walnut
308. Cheese and Tomato
309. Peanut Butter and Cucumber or Celery
310. Dried Fruit and Nut
311. Anchovy and Egg
312. Soya Flour and Peanut Butter

Open Sandwiches

313. Egg, Celery, Tomato and Ham
314. Scrambled Eggs and Chives
315. Tuna Fish, Sandwich Spread and Parsley
316. Marmite, Tomato and Cucumber

Party Snacks

317. Cheese and Celery Snacks
318. Banana and Bacon Rolls
319. Chicory and Pâté Boats
320. Bitter Balls

Sandwich Fillings

294. Cream Cheese and Red Pepper

4 oz. cream cheese	1 red pepper chopped small
2 oz. butter	1 tbs. chopped watercress
2 tbs. cream	sea salt and pepper

Cream butter and cheese together, stir in the cream and add the red pepper and watercress. Season carefully.

295. Sardine Spread

4 oz. tin of sardines	$\frac{1}{4}$ teasp. Worcester sauce
1 oz. butter	1 dsp. tomato sauce
1 dsp. lemon juice	sea salt and pepper

Mash sardines with butter, stir in the other ingredients and season to taste.

296. Nut and Raisin

$\frac{1}{4}$ lb. mixed nuts and raisins	$\frac{1}{2}$ oz. barbados sugar
1 teasp. mixed peel	2 teasp. lemon juice
1 oz. butter	

Wash and dry nuts and raisins. Chop finely with peel and stir in other ingredients.

297. Cream Cheese and Watercress

2 oz. cream cheese	1 dsp. chopped watercress
1 oz. butter	pinch of sea salt

Beat cheese and butter together to a soft cream then add the chopped watercress and seasoning.

298. Cream Cheese and Chutney

2 oz. cream cheese	1 teasp. chutney
1 oz. butter	sea salt and pepper

Beat cheese and butter together to a soft cream then stir in the chutney and the seasoning.

299. Sardine and Tomato

4 oz. sardines
½ lb. tomatoes

1 dsp. chopped parsley
sea salt and pepper

Mash sardines and skinned tomatoes, season well and add the chopped parsley.

300. Liver Pâté and Cucumber

4 oz. liver pâté
½ thinly sliced cucumber

sea salt and pepper

301. Ham, Eggs and Chives

3 oz. finely chopped ham
2 hard-boiled eggs
¼ oz. chopped chives

1 oz. butter
sea salt and pepper

Chop all ingredients and mix together with butter, salt and pepper.

302. Honey and Nuts

4 oz. peanuts or cashews

4 oz. thick honey

Grate nuts finely and mix with honey.

303. Marmite and Watercress

1 bundle watercress

1 oz. Marmite or Yeasty

Spread wholemeal bread with yeast extract, chop watercress finely and sprinkle on top.

304. Bacon

3 oz. streaky bacon

Grill bacon, cut into small pieces and sprinkle on wholemeal bread.

305. Cheese and Celery

2 oz. grated cheddar or danish   2 sticks of celery
   blue cheese   1 oz. butter

Chop celery very finely and mix with grated cheese using a little butter.

306. Curried Egg

2 hard-boiled eggs   1 oz. butter
1 teasp. curry powder

Chop eggs finely, mix with a little butter and add the curry powder.

307. Banana and Walnut

2 bananas   1 oz. walnuts

Mash bananas lightly, chop the walnuts and mix together.

308. Cheese and Tomato

2 oz. grated cheddar cheese   sea salt and pepper
¼ lb. tomatoes

Skin tomatoes and mash, add grated cheese, sea salt and pepper.

309. Peanut Butter and Cucumber or Celery

2 oz. peanut butter   ½ thinly sliced cucumber or
                             2 chopped sticks celery

Spread wholemeal bread with peanut butter and cover with cucumber or celery.

310. Dried Fruit and Nut

2 oz. raisins, dates or figs   1 oz. walnuts, cashews or pea-
                                                nuts

Mince fruit and nuts together and add a little water to make a paste.

311. Anchovy and Egg

2 hard-boiled eggs   few drops anchovy essence
1 oz. butter

Chop eggs with a little butter and add the anchovy essence.

312. Soya Flour and Peanut Butter

2 oz. peanut butter   ½ oz. mayonnaise (see page
½ oz. soya flour   11)

Blend ingredients together and spread.

Open Sandwiches

Cut rounds of wholemeal bread with scone cutter, spread with butter and:

313. Mix chopped hard-boiled eggs with mayonnaise (page 11) and arrange as outer ring on bread rounds, followed by a ring of chopped tomatoes and one of chopped celery. Put a little minced ham in the centre and a sprinkle of cayenne or parsley.

314. Scrambled eggs and chives.

315. Tuna fish with sandwich spread and parsley.

316. Marmite topped with sliced tomato and cucumber.

Party Snacks

317. Cheese and Celery Snacks

Fill celery sticks with a mixture of cream cheese and tomato sauce, cut into short lengths.

318. Banana and Bacon Rolls

Cut bananas in half crosswise. Roll each piece in half a bacon rasher and stick a skewer through the middle. Grill gently, turning so that the bacon cooks evenly. Remove the skewer and serve the rolls on hot buttered wholemeal toast slices.

319. Chicory and Pâté Boats

1 head of crisp chicory	1 tbs. sherry
4 oz. liver sausage	sea salt and pepper
2 tbs. milk	a few stuffed green olives

Skin liver sausage and mash with milk and sherry, season with sea salt and pepper and fill the separated chicory leaves with the paste. Decorate with sliced olives.

320. Bitter Balls

1 lb. stewing steak	pinch of nutmeg
1 oz. butter	dash of Maggi sauce
1½ oz. wholewheat flour	beaten eggs and wholewheat
½ pint beef stock or bouillon	breadcrumbs for coating
sea salt and pepper	vegetable oil for frying

Stew the meat gently until cooked. Melt the butter in a pan, add the flour and stir for several minutes. Put on one side to cool. Mince the cooked stewing steak. Add the hot beef stock to the butter and flour and stir until it is thick and creamy. Add the minced beef and seasonings and let it cool. When cool form the mixture into small balls, egg and breadcrumb them twice and fry in deep vegetable oil.

321. Cauliflower Fritters

1 cauliflower	1 egg white
2 oz. wholewheat flour	sea salt and pepper
2½ oz. water	spiced tomato sauce
1 dsp. vegetable oil	deep oil for frying

Wash and break cauliflower into small sprigs. Cook for 10 minutes in boiling salted water. Drain. Beat flour, water, vegetable oil and sea salt together and add the beaten egg white. Dip sprigs in batter and fry in deep oil until crisp and brown. Serve with bowl of spiced tomato sauce.

322. Cocktail Surprises

On cocktail sticks:
1. a cherry—a cube of cheese—a cocktail onion
2. an onion—a stoned cooked prune—a small roll of ham
3. two prawns—a chunk of cucumber
4. a cocktail sausage wrapped in a thin rasher of bacon
5. walnut halves stuck together with cream cheese

323. Party Titbits

1. Cooked prune stuffed with anchovy cream and an almond.
2. Cream cheese topped with a walnut half on a crouton or canapé of wholemeal bread.
3. Minced ham and chutney on a crouton.
4. Dates stuffed with grated cheddar cheese.
5. Grated cheese, grated onion, chopped chives, mustard, caraway seeds and paprika mixed together with cream and piled on potato crisps.
6. Anchovy butter spread on a crouton and topped with a shred of lettuce, a slice of cucumber, a slice of tomato and a small piece of anchovy.
7. Salted almonds. Blanche, skin and fry in butter; dip in sea salt.

324. Cheese and Nut Biscuits

8 oz. butter	2 oz. cheddar cheese
8 oz. wholewheat flour	beaten egg
2 oz. danish blue cheese	chopped cashews

Cut butter into flour, add the grated cheese and knead well together. Roll out, cut into biscuit shapes or strips. Brush with beaten egg and sprinkle with chopped nuts. Cook in oven 350 °F. (Reg. 4) for 15 minutes until golden brown.

325. Cucumber Rings

Slice cucumbers into 3-inch lengths. Remove seeds and fill with a mixture of cream cheese and crisp chopped bacon. Chill well. When required slice thinly and serve slices on pastry rounds or croutons.

326. Cheese Pastry

6 oz. wholewheat flour	2 oz. grated cheddar cheese
3 oz. butter	1 egg yolk
pinch of sea salt	

Rub the butter into the salted flour, add the cheese and bind into a stiff dough with egg yolk and cold water. Roll out thinly and cut into circles 3 inches in diameter. Cook in hot oven 450 °F. (Reg. 8) for 5 minutes.

Use cheese pastry for canapés and tartlets as a base for savoury fillings.

327. Cheese Straws

6 oz. wholewheat flour	4½ oz. grated cheddar cheese
4½ oz. butter	a little egg yolk
pinch of sea salt	cayenne

Rub butter into seasoned flour, add the cheese and mix to a stiff dough with a little egg yolk and water. Roll out and cut into strips, making some of them into rings, and bake in hot oven 450 °F. (Reg. 8) for 5–7 minutes. Serve straws in bundles pushed through the rings and the tips sprinkled with cayenne pepper.

328. Devilled Canapés

4 tbs. chopped cooked chicken	1 oz. wholewheat flour
6 oz. cheese pastry (see no. 326)	1 teasp. curry powder
	½ pint stock
1 small onion	1 teasp. tomato purée
1 oz. butter	cayenne

Roll out the cheese pastry thinly and cut into circles about 3 inches in diameter. Cook the chopped onion in the butter, add the curry powder then the flour. Stir until it has cooked for a little then add the stock and tomato purée slowly and simmer for 30 minutes. Stir in enough chicken to make a stiff mixture. Cook the pastry circles in a hot oven 450 °F. (Reg. 8) for 5 minutes. Pile mixture in pastry circles and sprinkle with cayenne.

329. Tomato Canapés

2 tomatoes	½ teasp. chopped onion
2 eggs	sea salt and pepper
1 oz. butter	cheese canapés (see no. 326)
2 oz. chopped ham	1 teasp. chopped parsley

Cook chopped onion in the butter, then add the ham, the tomatoes chopped finely and the seasoning. Cook for a few minutes then add the beaten eggs, stir until thick and allow to cool. Pile on to the canapés and sprinkle with finely chopped parsley.

330. Cheese Balls

4 oz. grated cheddar cheese	a little hot water
2 oz. finely chopped walnuts	

Mix the grated cheese with a little hot water until it is of a soft consistency. Add half the chopped walnuts and leave overnight. Next day roll into small balls and cover with chopped walnuts.

331. Savoury Butterflies

6 oz. cheese pastry (see no. 326)
1 oz. butter
2 oz. cream cheese
1 dsp. chopped watercress
sea salt and pepper

Roll out cheese pastry thinly and cut into circles about 3 inches in diameter. Cook in hot oven 450 °F. (Reg. 8) for 5 minutes. Cut some of them in half and allow to cool. Beat cream cheese and butter to a soft cream, add the chopped watercress and seasoning. Spread on cheese canapés, making a mound in the centre, and stick a half circle on each side to form wings.

332. Ham and Cheese Balls

½ lb. cooked chopped ham
5 oz. cream cheese
2 tbs. Worcester sauce
1 teasp. lemon juice
pepper

Mix all ingredients well together, form into balls and serve on cocktail sticks or potato crisps.

333. Paprika and Cheese Crackers

2 packets potato crisps
¼ small onion
1 dsp. chopped chives
2 tbs. cream cheese
1 tbs. cream
pinch dry mustard
pinch caraway seeds
sea salt and pepper
½ teasp. paprika

Chop the onion very finely and add to the cheese with the chives, caraway seeds and seasonings. Mix well and then add the cream and the paprika and beat well. Spread mixtures on potato crisps.

334. Cheese Crackers

Arrange thin salt biscuits in a baking tin, brush with melted butter, sprinkle with grated cheese and bake until the cheese melts.

335. Mushroom Fritters

Batter
2 oz. wholewheat flour
1 dsp. vegetable oil
1 egg
⅛ pint water

4 oz. mushrooms
sea salt and pepper
deep oil for frying
2 oz. butter

Cook mushrooms in butter, drain and slice. Mix into thick fritter batter. Drop tbs. of batter into hot deep oil and fry until golden brown.

Dips

To be served with Carrot sticks, Cauliflower sprigs, Potato crisps, Celery sticks, Cucumber chunks.

336. Leek and Nut Dip

4 oz. leek soup powder
2 cartons of yoghourt
2 oz. grated cheddar cheese

a sprinkle of paprika
1 oz. chopped walnuts

Mix the leek soup powder with the yoghourt and grated cheese and chill overnight. Sprinkle with paprika and chopped walnuts before serving.

337. Minestrone Dip

4 oz. minestrone soup powder
2 cartons yoghourt or soured cream

2 oz. grated cheddar cheese
2 tbs. chopped cucumber as garnish

Mix minestrone soup powder with cream and cheese and leave overnight in refrigerator. Garnish with chopped cucumber.

338. Celery Dip

4 oz. celery soup powder
2 cartons yoghourt or soured
  cream

2 oz. grated cheddar cheese
1 oz. chopped blanched
  almonds

Mix the soup powder with the cream or yoghourt and the cheese and chill overnight. Garnish with chopped blanched almonds before serving.

339. French Dip

8 oz. cottage cheese
4 oz. minced ham
1 tbs. horseradish sauce
4 tbs. cream
squeeze lemon juice

$\frac{1}{2}$ teasp. sea salt, shake of
  pepper
4 tbs. chopped watercress
1 teasp. grated onion

Blend all ingredients, chill well.

340. Yoghourt Dip

2 oz. cottage cheese
1 carton yoghourt
2 tbs. chopped celery
3 tbs. chopped onion

1 tbs. Worcester sauce
sea salt
1 tbs. chopped green pepper

Mix ingredients, chill, sprinkle with paprika.

10 - Bread, Scones, Cakes and Biscuits

377. Meringues
378. Brandy Snaps
379. Éclairs
380. Macaroons
381. Shortbread
382. Chocolate Shortbread
Biscuits
383. Chocolate Biscuit
Truffles
384. Chocolate Walnut
Cookies
385. Chocolate Crispies

386. Chocolate Sandwich
Slices
387. Peanut Butter Cookies
388. Almond Wedges
389. Coconut Biscuits
390. Lemon Tea Biscuits
391. Digestive Biscuits
392. Ginger Biscuits
393. Flapjacks
394. Coffee Biscuits
395. Nut Crispies
396. Japs
397. Honey Buns

341. Wholemeal Bread

1¼ lb. wholewheat flour
1 oz. butter
½ oz. barbados sugar
1 tbs. molasses or black
  treacle

¾ oz. dried yeast
¾ pint warm water
2 teasp. sea salt

Mix flour, salt and sugar in a large bowl. Melt the butter
slowly, add the molasses. Dissolve the yeast in a little warm
water then add to the flour followed by the butter and the
molasses. Mix with your left hand whilst pouring in the warm
water with the right. Turn out on to a floured board and knead
well for about 15 minutes. Put the mixture back into the bowl,
cover and leave for 1 hour. Turn out on to board again and
knead lightly for a few minutes. Place in greased loaf tin and
leave to prove for a further 45 minutes before baking in a hot
oven 425 °F. (Reg. 7) for 25 minutes and at 350 °F. (Reg. 4)
for a further 25 minutes.

342. Fruit Bread

4 oz. self-raising wholewheat
  flour
1 tbs. barbados sugar
1 tbs. black treacle

5 tbs. freshly brewed tea
1 egg
1 oz. butter
3 oz. mixed dried fruit

Mix the treacle, sugar, egg, butter and hot tea together and
stir until blended. Add to the flour, mixing well and sprinkling
in the fruit. When mixture is well mixed pour into greased
loaf tin and bake for 45 minutes in oven 350 °F. (Reg. 4). Slice
and spread with butter when cool.

343. Date and Walnut Loaf

4 oz. dates
4 oz. boiling water
1 oz. butter or margarine
3 oz. barbados sugar

1 egg
1 oz. chopped walnuts
4 oz. self-raising wholewheat
  flour

Chop the dates, pour over the boiling water and leave to get cool. Cream butter and sugar. Add the egg, the date mixture and the walnuts. Mix well then add the flour. Pour the mixture into a greased and lined loaf tin and bake for 1 hour in oven 350 °F. (Reg. 4).

344. Irish Bread

12 oz. mixed dried fruit
4 oz. barbados sugar
½ cup cold tea
1 egg
1 tbs. marmalade

2 teasp. mixed spice
8 oz. self-raising wholewheat
flour
sea salt

Put the mixed dried fruit and the sugar into a bowl, pour the cold tea over them and leave overnight. Stir in the egg, marmalade and spice. Add the flour with a little sea salt, pour mixture into a greased and lined 2 lb. loaf tin and cook for 1 hour in oven 375 °F. (Reg. 5).

345. Honey Bread

6 oz. self-raising wholewheat
flour
3 oz. barbados sugar
1 oz. butter

6 oz. milk
1 teasp. ground cinnamon
½ teasp. sea salt
2 tbs. honey

Mix all the dry ingredients. Heat the butter, honey and milk in a small pan, stirring constantly until well blended. Stir into the dry ingredients and mix well. Pour into a greased and floured small loaf tin and cook in oven 375 °F. (Reg. 5) for 1 hour.

346. Nut Peel Bread

12 oz. self-raising wholewheat
flour
1 teasp. sea salt
2 oz. chopped walnuts
5 oz. milk

2 oz. chopped candied peel
4 oz. barbados sugar
2 eggs
2 oz. butter

Mix dry ingredients in a large bowl. Add the eggs, milk and melted butter. Stir well and pour into greased 2 lb. loaf tin and cook in oven 350 °F. (Reg. 4) for 1 hour.

347. Allbran Loaf

1 cup Allbran	1 cup self-raising wholewheat
1 cup barbados sugar	flour
1 cup sultanas	1 egg
1 cup milk	

Put all ingredients except flour and egg into a large bowl and leave overnight. Next morning beat in the egg and the flour. Pour mixture into well-greased loaf tin and bake in oven 350 °F. (Reg. 4) for 1 hour.

348. Treacle Loaf

8 oz. self-raising wholewheat flour	$\frac{1}{2}$ gill milk
1 teasp. sea salt	2 oz. barbados sugar
1 teasp. mixed spice	2 tbs. black treacle
2 oz. butter	4 oz. seeded raisins
	1 egg

Place butter, milk, sugar, treacle and raisins in a saucepan and warm gently until the butter is melted. Mix flour, spice and salt in a large bowl. Add the egg then the cooled milk mixture. Mix thoroughly, pour into greased loaf tin and cook in oven 350 °F. (Reg. 4) for 45 minutes.

349. Banana Bread

$2\frac{1}{2}$ oz. butter	7 oz. self-raising wholewheat
5 oz. barbados sugar	flour
1 teasp. grated lemon rind	3 ripe bananas
	2 eggs

Cream the butter, sugar and lemon rind. Mash the bananas and mix with beaten eggs. Fold the flour into the butter mixture alternately with the banana mixture. Beat until smooth. Pour into well-greased and floured tin and cook in oven 350 °F. (Reg. 4) for 1 hour.

350. Wholemeal Scones

8 oz. self-raising wholewheat flour	1 egg
	1 teasp. syrup
1 teasp. sea salt	1 tbs. warm water
1 oz. lard	1 teacup milk
1 oz. margarine	

Rub fat into salted flour. Add beaten egg, then syrup dissolved in warm water, then the milk. Mix into soft dough and turn out on to floured board. Roll out to $\frac{3}{4}$ inch thick and cut into triangles or rounds. Put on greased baking tray, brush the tops with milk and bake in top of hot oven 450 °F. (Reg. 8) for 10–15 minutes.

351. Wholemeal Fruit Scones

8 oz. self-raising wholewheat flour	2 oz. sultanas
	2 oz. barbados sugar
1 teasp. sea salt	1 teacup milk
2 oz. margarine	1 egg

Rub fat into salted flour, add sultanas and sugar then the milk and beaten egg. Mix to a soft dough then turn out on to floured board. Roll out to $\frac{3}{4}$ inch thick and cut into rounds. Brush tops with milk; place on greased tray and bake in hot oven 450 °F. (Reg. 8) for 15 minutes.

352. Drop Scones

8 oz. self-raising wholewheat flour	$\frac{1}{2}$ teasp. sea salt
	$\frac{1}{4}$ pint milk
2 eggs	$\frac{1}{2}$ oz. melted butter
1 oz. barbados sugar	

Mix dry ingredients, drop the eggs into a well in the centre
with half the milk. Beat well and then add the rest of the milk
and the melted butter. Beat for another few minutes and then
drop spoonfuls on to a hot greased girdle or heavy frying pan.
Turn when bubbles appear and cook on the other side. Spread
with plenty of butter.

353. Hot Cross Buns

1 lb. plain wholewheat flour	2 oz. chopped candied peel
1 teasp. sea salt	4 oz. currants
1 teasp. mixed spice	1½ oz. barbados sugar
½ teasp. powdered cinnamon	1 egg
1 oz. yeast	milk to mix (tepid)
2 oz. margarine or butter	

Mix the flour, cinnamon, sea salt and mixed spice. Rub in the
margarine or butter, then add the sugar and the cleaned fruit.
Make a well in the centre of the mixture. Mix the yeast with
the tepid milk and a little sugar and pour into the well together
with beaten egg. Add sufficient milk to make a soft dough.
Knead thoroughly and leave to rise till the dough has doubled
its size. Turn on to a floured board and knead well. Divide
into 12 pieces. Shape each piece into a bun, mark with a cross
and place on well-greased baking trays. Leave in a warm place
to rise for 25 minutes. Dissolve 1 tbs. sugar in 1 tbs. milk by
bringing to the boil gently and boiling carefully for 1 minute
until syrupy. Brush the buns with this glaze and bake in hot
oven 450 °F. (Reg. 8) for 15–20 minutes. Brush the buns with
the glaze again as soon as they are removed from the oven.

354. Ginger Cake

1 lb. self-raising wholewheat flour	2 oz. crystallized ginger
	4 oz. chopped walnuts
pinch sea salt	8 oz. butter
2 teasp. mixed spice	2 tbs. syrup
3 teasp. ground ginger	2 tbs. black treacle or molasses
6 oz. barbados sugar	2 eggs
6 oz. sultanas	1 teacupful milk

Put salted flour and spices into basin and add sugar, chopped ginger, sultanas and nuts and mix well. Melt butter, syrup and treacle together very gently until the butter has melted. Pour mixture into middle of flour mixture and add the beaten eggs. Add the milk all at once and mix thoroughly. Pour into greased and lined deep cake or loaf tin. Place in centre of low oven 325 °F. (Reg. 3) for 2 hours. Allow to cool in tin.

355. Rich Chocolate Layer Cake

4 oz. plain chocolate	10 oz. self-raising wholewheat flour
4 oz. barbados sugar	
⅓ pint milk	pinch sea salt
1 egg yolk	1 gill milk
3 egg whites	
4 oz. demerara sugar	*Butter icing*
3 oz. butter	2 oz. milk powder
2 well-beaten egg yolks	2 oz. cocoa
	8 oz. butter
	4 oz. barbados sugar

Melt the plain chocolate in the top of a double saucepan. Add the barbados sugar and ⅓ pint milk and the slightly beaten egg yolk. Cook this mixture over hot water until it is smooth, then leave to cool. Beat three egg whites until they are stiff; then beat in 4 oz. demerara sugar and put on one side.

Cream the butter and 4 oz. demerara sugar and add the two well-beaten egg yolks. Put the flour into a basin with a pinch of sea salt. Add the butter mixture to the flour alternately with the gill of milk. Add the chocolate mixture and beat well. Finally fold in the beaten egg whites. Put into two buttered and floured 7-inch tins and bake in oven 350 °F. (Reg. 4) for 35 minutes. When cool slice each cake in two and sandwich all four layers together with chocolate butter icing.

356. Chocolate Honey Cake

3 oz. unsweetened chocolate
8 tbs. clear honey
6 oz. self-raising wholewheat flour
1 teasp. sea salt
4 oz. butter
3 oz. barbados sugar
1 teasp. vanilla essence

2 eggs
$\frac{1}{4}$ pint water

Icing
6 oz. chocolate
4 tbs. honey
4 oz. barbados sugar
2 oz. powdered milk
2 tbs. warm water

Melt the chocolate and the honey in a double saucepan. Cool. Cream butter and sugar, add eggs one by one and stir into the chocolate mixture with the vanilla essence. Add salted flour alternately with $\frac{1}{4}$ pint water, beat well and pour into two greased and floured sandwich tins. Bake in oven 350 °F. (Reg. 4) for 45 minutes.

Make icing by melting the honey and chocolate as for the cake, cool slightly and beat in 4 oz. barbados sugar, 2 tbs. warm water and 2 oz. powdered milk. Sandwich the layers together with this mixture and spread the rest over the cake.

357. Chocolate Slices

8 oz. demerara sugar
$1\frac{1}{2}$ oz. cocoa
3 oz. self-raising wholewheat flour
4 oz. melted butter

1 teasp. sea salt
2 eggs
2 tbs. milk
3 oz. chopped walnuts
8 oz. cooking chocolate

Mix all the dry ingredients together in a large basin. Add the melted butter, milk and the beaten eggs. Stir well, pour into

173

a tin measuring 9 × 12 inches and bake in oven 350 °F. (Reg. 4) for 30 minutes. Cool in tin and cut into slices. Spread with melted chocolate.

358. Coffee Cake

4 oz. butter	*Coffee syrup*
3 oz. barbados sugar	¼ pint water
4 oz. self-raising wholewheat flour	4 oz. barbados sugar
2 eggs	½ gill black coffee or rum or brandy
2 tbs. coffee essence or 1 tbs. Nescafé	½ pint double cream
	flaked almonds

Cream butter and sugar together, add the eggs gradually then the essence and the flour. Turn into greased and floured cake tin and bake in oven 350 °F. (Reg. 4) for 35 minutes. Prepare the syrup by boiling water and sugar together slowly for 1–2 minutes. Draw aside and add the coffee and/or the spirit. When cake is cool return to tin, pour over it the syrup and leave overnight. Turn out the next day and smother the top with whipped cream and flaked almonds.

359. Hazel Nut Cake

1½ oz. hazel nuts	*Filling*
3 oz. butter	2 apples
2 oz. barbados sugar	1 tbs. thick honey
1 egg plus 1 white	grated rind and juice of 1 lemon
1 tbs. coffee essence	
3 oz. self-raising wholewheat flour	*Icing*
2 tbs. milk	4 oz. chocolate
	2 tbs. water
	8 walnut halves

Skin and chop the hazel nuts. Cream butter and sugar and gradually add one beaten egg; add the coffee essence. Fold in the flour and the chopped hazel nuts with the milk. Fold in the extra egg white whipped stiff. Divide the mixture between two greased and floured tins and bake in oven 350 °F. (Reg. 4) for ½ hour. Turn out and allow to cool.

Peel core and slice the apples and cook with the honey, lemon rind and juice until tender. When cool, sandwich the two halves of the cake with this filling. Melt the chocolate with the water in a double saucepan and pour over the cake. Decorate with walnut halves.

360. Coffee Slices

3 eggs
3 oz. barbados sugar
1½ oz. ground almonds
1 oz. dried wholewheat
   breadcrumbs
3½ oz. self-raising wholewheat
   flour

1 gill black coffee
vanilla essence
whipped cream

Icing

8 oz. barbados sugar
4 tbs. black coffee
2 oz. butter

Beat the egg yolks with the sugar. Mix the flour, breadcrumbs and ground almonds. Add these dry ingredients to the egg yolks and sugar alternately with the black coffee. Add the vanilla essence. Whisk the egg whites until they are stiff and fold them into the mixture. Spread this mixture on greased shallow tin and bake in oven 350 °F. (Reg. 4) for 20 minutes.

Melt 2 oz. of barbados sugar in the black coffee and bring to the boil stirring all the time. Cool, then add the remainder of the sugar and the butter and beat until smooth and creamy. Sandwich the layers together with whipped cream and pour the icing over the whole cake. Cut in slices.

361. Orange Sponge Cake

4 oz. ground almonds	*Icing*
4 oz. self-raising wholewheat flour	3 oz. butter
	3 oz. barbados sugar
3 oz. barbados sugar	2 oz. powdered milk
3 eggs	juice and rind of 1 orange
2 oranges	

Beat sugar and egg yolks together, add the ground almonds and juice and grated rind of the oranges. Fold in the flour then the stiffly beaten egg whites. Pour into greased tin and cook in oven 375 °F. (Reg. 5) for 15 minutes.

Make butter icing by beating together the butter and sugar, adding the powdered milk, and finally the rind and juice of 1 orange. Slice cake in half when cool, and sandwich the halves together with the butter icing. Decorate the top with the remainder of the butter icing and place orange quarter slices round the edge.

362. Dundee Cake

6 oz. currants	6 oz. plain wholewheat flour
6 oz. sultanas	pinch sea salt
2 oz. chopped mixed peel	1 teasp. mixed spice
1 oz. glacé cherries	1 tbs. milk
6 oz. barbados sugar	1 tbs. brandy
6 oz. butter	2 oz. blanched almonds
4 eggs	

Cream the butter and the sugar; add the eggs, dried fruit, flour, salt and spice. Mix well, add the milk and the brandy. Pour into greased and lined tin, place the blanched almonds on the top. Cook in oven 350 °F. (Reg. 4) for 1 hour and for a further ¾ hour at 300 °F. (Reg. 2–3).

363. Cherry Cake

6 oz. butter
4 oz. barbados sugar
6 oz. self-raising wholewheat flour

3 eggs
1 teasp. grated lemon rind
6 oz. glacé cherries

Cream butter and sugar, add the lemon rind then the beaten eggs. Cut cherries in half and coat them in flour. Fold the flour and the cherries into the mixture; do not beat. Pour into a greased and lined tin and bake in oven 375 °F. (Reg. 5) for 50–60 minutes.

364. Rich Christmas Cake or Wedding Cake

12 oz. sultanas
1 lb. currants
12 oz. stoned raisins
8 oz. glacé cherries
4 oz. chopped mixed peel
grated rind of 1 lemon
8 eggs
4 oz. nibbed almonds

1 lb. 2 oz. wholewheat flour
1 teasp. ground cinnamon
$\frac{1}{2}$ teasp. ground mace
15 oz. butter
15 oz. barbados sugar
4 tbs. brandy
1 greased and double lined 9-inch cake tin

Cream butter and sugar together with a wooden spoon in a large bowl. Add the beaten eggs gradually, beating well between additions. Add a little flour if mixture shows signs of curdling. Wash and clean the fruit and chop the cherries into small pieces. Fold into the mixture alternately with the flour. Fold in the lemon rind, mixed peel, cinnamon, mace and the nuts and mix thoroughly. Add 2 tbs. of the brandy and pour mixture into prepared tin, make a slight hollow in the middle to prevent uneven rising. Put tin on a baking tin lined with thick brown paper and bake in oven 300 °F. (Reg. 2) for $4\frac{1}{2}$ hours. When cool prick base and top of cake with skewer and spoon over the extra 2 tbs. brandy. Wrap in greaseproof paper then place in airtight tin and store for one month.

365. Almond Paste

1 lb. barbados sugar
1 lb. ground almonds
juice of 1 lemon
1 teasp. orange flower water

1 teasp. vanilla essence
2 egg yolks
honey

Mix the sugar and the ground almonds. Add the lemon juice, essences and enough egg yolk to bind the ingredients into a pliable but dry paste. Knead thoroughly until smooth. Brush cake with warm honey before applying the almond paste.

366. Frosted Icing

1 lb. demerara sugar
8 tbs. water

2 egg whites

Put the sugar and the water in a saucepan and dissolve the sugar very slowly. When dissolved bring mixture to boiling point and boil to 240 °F. or until a little dropped in cold water forms a ball when rolled between thumb and forefinger. Brush down the side of the pan with a brush dipped in cold water and remove scum. Pour mixture on to stiffly beaten egg whites beating all the time. Continue beating until icing begins to thicken. Pour over cake and whip up with palette-knife.

367. Walnut Fudge Cake

4 oz. butter
4 oz. barbados sugar
1 egg
1 dsp. cocoa powder

½ lb. crushed biscuit crumbs
1 oz. chopped walnuts
whipped cream

Melt fat and sugar in a pan, add the cocoa and bring to the boil. Remove from the heat and beat in the egg, crushed biscuits and the nuts. Press mixture into sandwich cake tin and leave to set. Turn out carefully and decorate with whipped cream.

368. Praline Cream Party Cake

8 oz. butter
6 oz. barbados sugar
4 eggs
10 oz. self-raising wholewheat
 flour
1 oz. ground almonds
1–2 tbs. water
4 oz. thick honey

nibbed almonds
whipped cream

Praline cream
1 oz. ground almonds
4 oz. demerara sugar
¼ pint water
3 egg yolks
¼ pint double cream

Cream butter and sugar together and gradually beat in the eggs one by one. Add the flour and the ground almonds and stir in the water. Mix well then pour into greased and lined 10-inch cake tin and bake for 1¼ hours in oven 350 °F. (Reg. 4).

Praline Cream: Spread the ground almonds on a baking tray and bake until golden brown. Allow to cool. Dissolve the sugar slowly in ¼ pint water in a small thick saucepan, then boil carefully until a little dropped in cold water forms a firm ball when rolled between thumb and forefinger. Pour this over the egg yolks whisking continuously. Stir in the roasted ground almonds and continue to whisk until the mixture begins to thicken and cool. When cold fold in ¼ pint whipped cream.

Split cake in two, spread lower half with a little warm honey then spread a good layer of praline cream on top and replace the top half of the cake. Coat the top and sides of the cake with praline cream. Scatter almond nibs round the sides of the cake and decorate the top with piped lines of fresh cream and praline cream with almonds in between.

369. Honey Cake

10 oz. butter
13 oz. clear honey
6 eggs
3 oz. barbados sugar

1 lb. self-raising wholewheat
 flour
1 teasp. ground ginger
1 teasp. ground cloves

Cream the butter and honey together. Beat in the eggs gradually. Add the sugar and beat lightly. Mix flour and spices together and fold into the mixture. Bake in a greased oblong tin in oven 350 °F. (Reg. 4) for 1 hour. (If left in a tin for 2–3 weeks before eating this cake becomes soft and sticky.)

370. Orange and Lemon Cake

1 lemon
1 orange
6 oz. butter
4 oz. barbados sugar
3 eggs
6 oz. self-raising wholewheat
  flour

Butter icing
8 oz. butter
4 oz. barbados sugar
2 oz. powdered milk
orange rind and lemon juice

Grate the rind of the orange into the lemon juice and leave for 1 hour.

Cream the butter and sugar together and gradually add the beaten eggs. Add the juice of the orange, fold in the flour and mix well. Bake in oven 375 °F. (Reg. 5) for 25 minutes, in two greased sandwich tins.

Make butter icing by creaming barbados sugar and butter together then adding the powdered milk and the lemon juice and orange rind. When the cakes are cool sandwich them together with this icing and spread it over the top. Decorate with thin slices of orange and lemon.

371. Basic Butter Sponge Cake

6 oz. butter
4 oz. barbados sugar
3 eggs

6 oz. self-raising wholewheat
  flour
2 tbs. boiling water

Cream butter and sugar until the mixture is light and fluffy. Add the well-beaten eggs alternately with the flour, beating lightly, then add the boiling water. Bake in oven 350 °F. (Reg. 4) for 20–25 minutes.

Bread, Scones, Cakes and Biscuits

372. Banana Layer Cake

2½ oz. butter	*Butter cream*
4 oz. barbados sugar	4 oz. butter
2 eggs	1 egg white
6 oz. self-raising wholewheat flour	4 oz. demerara sugar
3 mashed bananas	1 teasp. liqueur
2 tbs. milk	2 bananas

Cream the butter and sugar. Add beaten eggs gradually. Combine milk and mashed bananas and add to the mixture alternately with the flour. Pour into two greased sandwich tins and bake in oven 400 °F. (Reg. 6) for 25 minutes.

Butter Cream: Cream the butter thoroughly, then add the whisked up egg white by the spoonful. Beat in the sugar gradually and flavour with 1 teasp. liqueur. Sandwich halves together with this cream and sliced bananas and decorate top of cake in the same manner.

373. Honey Boats

2 oz. wholewheat flour	*Filling*
pinch sea salt	4 oz. butter
1 oz. barbados sugar	3 oz. barbados sugar
1 oz. butter	4 oz. ground almonds
1 egg yolk	3 teasp. thick honey
	2 teasp. coffee essence
	whipped cream

To make the sweet pastry, put the salted flour on a board or marble slab, make a well in the centre and into it put the butter, sugar and egg yolk. Work the butter, sugar and yolk with the fingertips until they are well blended. Work in the flour and knead lightly until smooth. Put in a cool place for at least 1 hour. Roll out and line 8 boat-shaped patty tins with the paste and bake blind in oven 375 °F. (Reg. 5) for 5–7 minutes. Cool on wire rack.

Cream the butter and sugar until light and fluffy, beat in the almonds, honey and essence. Fill the pasty boats and chill. Decorate with whipped cream.

374. Almond Topped Biscuits

4 oz. self-raising wholewheat flour	½ teasp. ground ginger
2 oz. butter	1 egg yolk
2 oz. barbados sugar	milk to mix
	2 oz. whole almonds

Rub fat, sugar and flour together. Add ginger and stir in the egg yolk. Add a little milk if necessary to make a stiff dough. Roll out to ½ inch thickness and cut into biscuit shapes with cutter. Blanch the almonds and place one on top of each biscuit. Place biscuits on baking tray and bake for about 20 minutes in oven 350 °F. (Reg. 4).

375. Coffee Nut Biscuits

4 oz. wholewheat flour	¼ teasp. vanilla essence
¼ teasp. sea salt	½ oz. finely ground coffee
1½ oz. butter	2 tbs. cornflakes
2 oz. barbados sugar	water to mix

Rub butter into salted flour. Add sugar, essence, coffee and cornflakes. Stir in enough water to make a stiff paste. Roll out and cut in 2-inch rounds. Bake in oven 400 °F. (Reg. 5) for 20 minutes.

376. Peanut Biscuits

6 oz. barbados sugar	1 cup shelled chopped peanuts
8 oz. butter	1 egg
8 oz. self-raising wholewheat flour	

Cream butter and sugar. Add beaten egg gradually, then the nuts. Fold in the flour to make a stiff dough. Put small mounds

on greased baking tray and bake in oven 350 °F. (Reg. 4) for
15 minutes.

377. Meringues

2 egg whites   4 oz. demerara sugar

Beat egg whites until stiff then beat in half the sugar and whisk
until mixture is really stiff again, then fold in the rest of the
sugar with a cool metal spoon. Line greased baking tray with
two layers of oiled greaseproof paper and pipe meringue mixture in mounds on to the oiled paper. Dry off for 2–3 hours in
oven at lowest number. Turn over and dry off for a further
hour. Store in airtight tins until required, then sandwich together with whipped cream and serve.

378. Brandy Snaps

2 oz. butter or margarine   2 oz. wholewheat flour
2 oz. demerara sugar   ½ teasp. ground ginger
1 tbs. syrup   1 teasp. brandy or rum
1 tbs. black treacle or molasses   ½ teasp. grated lemon rind

Melt butter, sugar, syrup and treacle in a saucepan. Remove
from heat and stir in the other ingredients until they are well
mixed together. Drop mixture in teaspoonfuls on to a greased
baking tray about 2 inches apart. Bake in moderate oven
350 °F. (Reg. 4) for 7–10 minutes until golden brown. Lift the
biscuits off with a palette-knife and roll them round greased
wooden spoon handles. When they are cold slip them off carefully. If the biscuits get too hard to lift off the tray place it over
the heat for a minute and they will come off easily. Fill them
with whipped cream.

379. Éclairs

4 oz. butter or margarine	pinch of sea salt
2 pints water	½ teasp. vanilla essence
8 oz. wholewheat flour	½ pint whipped cream
6 eggs	8 oz. chocolate

Put water, butter and salt in a pan and bring to the boil. Remove from heat and add the flour all at once. Beat hard with a wooden spoon over a very low heat until smooth. Allow to cool a little then add the beaten eggs and ½ teasp. vanilla essence and continue beating until smooth and creamy. Pipe on to greased baking tray and bake in oven 375 °F. (Reg. 5) for 20–25 minutes. Split down one side to allow to cool and fill with whipped cream. Coat tops with melted chocolate.

380. Macaroons

4 oz. ground almonds	2 teasp. water
6 oz. demerara sugar	rice paper
2 egg whites	blanched almonds for decora-
½ oz. cornflour	tion
3 drops vanilla essence	

Put the ground almonds and the sugar into a basin and add the unbeaten egg whites. Beat for 1 minute. Add the cornflour, vanilla essence and water. Line a flat baking tray with rice paper. Place the mixture in a piping bag with a plain ½-inch pipe and pipe on to the rice paper, allowing room for spreading. Brush with a little egg white and place a blanched almond on top of each one. Bake in oven 375 °F. (Reg. 5) for 15 minutes. Tear the rice paper round each macaroon and cool on wire tray.

381. Shortbread

8 oz. wholewheat flour	5 oz. demerara sugar
6 oz. butter	a pinch of sea salt

Rub the butter into the salted flour. Add the sugar. Knead with the hands until the mixture is soft. Sprinkle a little sugar on a board and roll out the mixture to ½ inch thick. Cut into fingers, put on a baking tray and bake in oven 375 °F. (Reg. 5) for 20 minutes or until golden brown.

382. Chocolate Shortbread Biscuits

2 oz. butter
2 oz. barbados sugar
2 oz. wholewheat flour

1 oz. ground almonds
1 oz. grated chocolate
few drops vanilla essence

Cream butter and sugar, beat in the remaining ingredients, knead for a few minutes then roll out thinly. Cut into small rounds and bake in oven 350 °F. (Reg. 4) for 10 minutes. When cold sandwich together with chocolate nut cream.

Chocolate nut cream: 1 oz. butter, 1 oz. barbados sugar, 1 oz. grated chocolate, 1 oz. finely chopped walnuts. Cream butter and sugar then add the other ingredients and mix well. Pour melted chocolate over the top of the biscuits.

383. Chocolate Biscuit Truffles

4 oz. plain chocolate
4 oz. cake or biscuit crumbs
1 wineglass sherry

2 oz. thick honey
¼ pint double cream
frilled paper cake cases

Melt the chocolate, turn it on to a slab and work for a few minutes with a knife; then, still using the knife, cover the inside of the cake cases with a thin layer of chocolate. When quite set peel off the paper and fill the bottom of the chocolate cases with cake or biscuit crumbs soaked in sherry. Cover with honey and top with whipped cream.

384. Chocolate Walnut Cookies

4 oz. butter
2 oz. barbados sugar
2 tbs. water

4 oz. wholewheat flour
2 oz. chopped walnuts
4 oz. chopped chocolate

Cream together the butter, sugar and water. Add the dry ingredients and mix well. Drop in teaspoonfuls on baking tray and cook for 12 minutes in oven 350 °F. (Reg. 4).

385. Chocolate Crispies

4 oz. butter	2 oz. chopped glacé cherries
4 oz. barbados sugar	4 oz. rice crispies
2 oz. chopped dates	8 oz. plain chocolate

Melt the butter and sugar over gentle heat for a few minutes, then add the dates and the cherries and cook for a few minutes longer. Stir in the rice crispies, stir well and then press into oblong tin and cover with melted chocolate. Cut into strips when set.

386. Chocolate Sandwich Slices

6 oz. wholewheat flour	1 egg yolk
2 tbs. cocoa	1 tbs. milk
4 oz. butter	4 oz. plain chocolate
4 oz. barbados sugar	

Mix flour and cocoa, rub in the butter and add the sugar. Mix to a dough with the beaten egg yolk and the milk. Roll out thinly and cut into small slices. Bake in oven 350 °F. (Reg. 4) for 15 minutes. When cold sandwich together with melted chocolate.

387. Peanut Butter Cookies

4 oz. butter	4 oz. wholewheat flour
4 oz. peanut butter	$\frac{1}{2}$ teasp. vanilla essence
6 oz. barbados sugar	pinch sea salt
1 egg	

Cream together the butter, sugar and peanut butter. Work in the egg, then add the rest of the ingredients. Arrange in heaped teaspoonfuls on greased baking tray and press flat with fork. Bake in oven 350 °F. (Reg. 4) for 10 minutes.

388. Almond Wedges

4 oz. butter
4 oz. demerara sugar

8 oz. quick-cooking porridge
oats
few drops of almond essence

Melt sugar in the butter over gentle heat. Stir in the oats and
the almond essence. Press into well-greased oblong tray and
bake in oven 350 °F. (Reg. 4) for ½ hour. Cut into wedges
whilst still hot but do not remove until cold as they break
easily.

389. Coconut Biscuits

8 oz. butter
8 oz. wholewheat flour
6 oz. barbados sugar

8 oz. desiccated coconut
1 egg

Rub butter into flour and add the sugar and the desiccated
coconut. Mix to a paste with the beaten egg. Roll out thinly
and cut into biscuit shapes and bake in oven 350 °F. (Reg. 4)
for 10 minutes.

390. Lemon Tea Biscuits

4 oz. butter
8 oz. wholewheat flour
4 oz. barbados sugar
grated rind of 1 lemon

2 eggs
2 oz. chopped blanched and
roasted almonds

Rub the butter into the flour and add the sugar and the lemon
rind. Mix to a dough with the two well-whipped eggs. Roll out
on floured board and sprinkle with the chopped almonds.
Stamp into rounds with a cutter and bake in oven 350 °F.
(Reg. 4) for about 10 minutes.

391. Digestive Biscuits

8 oz. wholewheat flour   2 oz. butter
8 oz. medium oatmeal   2 oz. syrup
2 oz. demerara sugar   a little milk

Mix dry ingredients, rub in the butter and add the melted syrup and a little milk if necessary. Roll out, cut in biscuit shapes with cutter, prick with a skewer and bake in oven 350 °F. (Reg. 4) for 20 minutes.

392. Ginger Biscuits

1 tbs. syrup   6 oz. barbados sugar
2 tbs. boiling water   pinch sea salt
3 oz. butter   2 teasp. ground ginger
8 oz. self-raising wholewheat
  flour

Mix dry ingredients, rub in the butter then add the syrup mixed with the boiling water. Put in small mounds on a greased baking tray and cook in oven 300 °F. (Reg. 1–2) for ½ hour.

393. Flapjacks

5 oz. butter or margarine   1 oz. black treacle
3 oz. barbados sugar   8 oz. quick porridge oats
1 oz. syrup   rind and juice of 1 lemon

Melt the butter, sugar, syrup and treacle in a saucepan over low heat stirring all the time. Add the oats, lemon rind and juice and mix well. Spread mixture over shallow greased baking tray and bake in oven 400 °F. (Reg. 6) for 25 minutes.

For variations sprinkle desiccated coconut over the top just before baking or chopped walnuts. They can also be iced with melted plain chocolate.

394. Coffee Biscuits

2 eggs

1 teasp. coffee essence

2 oz. demerara sugar

2 oz. wholewheat flour

2 oz. thin honey

2 oz. chopped almonds

Whisk two egg whites until very light and frothy; whisk in the coffee essence and the sugar. Beat for 5 minutes then lightly fold in the flour. Pour mixture into flat tin lined with greased paper. Bake in oven 350 °F. (Reg. 4) for 15 minutes approx. Cut into slices with sharp knife and coat with thin honey and chopped almonds.

395. Nut Crispies

2 oz. butter

2 oz. demerara sugar

1 oz. syrup

2 oz. rice crispies or cornflakes

2 oz. chopped walnuts or hazelnuts

Melt butter with sugar and syrup over gentle heat, boil for a minute or two stirring all the time, then add the crispies or cornflakes and the chopped nuts. Mix well and then form into small pyramids and put into paper cases.

396. Japs

4 egg whites

½ lb. demerara sugar

½ lb. ground almonds

few drops almond essence

Butter icing

2 oz. butter

2 oz. barbados sugar

1 oz. dried milk powder

coffee essence

Whisk the egg whites until they are stiff, shower in half the sugar and whisk again. Fold in the rest of the sugar and the ground almonds and the almond essence. Spread the mixture on well-oiled and floured tins and bake in oven 350 °F. (Reg. 4) until almost set. Remove from the oven and mark into rounds of 1½ inches with a cutter, then return to the oven and continue to cook until quite firm. Remove the rounds from the tray and put them on a wire rack to cool.

Continue to cook the left-over trimmings until really crisp and dry. Crush with a rolling pin and pass through a sieve.

Make the butter icing and sandwich the biscuits together, smoothing the surplus filling round the sides and over the top and bottom. Dip in the sieved trimmings and decorate the top with a chocolate drop or a crystallized flower petal.

397. Honey Buns

2 tbs. honey	2 oz. mixed peel
2 oz. barbados sugar	1½ oz. ground almonds
8 oz. plain wholewheat flour	a pinch each of cinnamon,
2 oz. butter	nutmeg, cloves, mixed spice
2 eggs	

Melt honey and sugar in 1 tbs. water. Pour into a bowl and stir in the flour. Stir in the melted butter alternately with the beaten eggs. Stir in the other ingredients. Leave in the refrigerator overnight. Next morning roll out the dough to ½ inch thickness. Cut into shapes with biscuit cutters. Bake in oven 350 °F. (Reg. 4) for 15 minutes.

11- Herbs and Spices

Allspice

Basil

Bay Leaves

Caraway Seed

Cayenne Pepper

Celery Salt

Chilli Powder

Chives

Cinnamon

Cloves

Cumin Seed

Curry Powder

Garlic Salt

Ginger

Mace

Marjoram

Mint

Mixed Spice

Nutmeg

Paprika

Parsley

Rosemary

Sage

Tarragon

Thyme

Turmeric

Bouquet Garni

Herbs and Spices

Allspice

Spicy, sweet and mild. Used whole in pickles, chutney and stews.

Basil

A mild, sweet and pungent herb. Used in all tomato dishes, with cold rice salads, in egg sandwiches and with liver and lamb.

Bay Leaves

A herb with a mild and distinctive flavour. Used in soups, stews, marinades, in boiling ox tongue, soused herrings, meat and fish casseroles. Add to milk when heating for sweet and savoury white sauces.

Caraway Seed

Pleasant, slightly sharp flavour. Used in rye bread, seed cake, veal dishes, cheese spreads, and with pork and goose.

Cayenne Pepper

Hot pungent flavour. Used in devilled dishes, in fish cakes, and many cheese dishes.

Celery Salt

Celery flavoured salt. Useful for flavouring stews and casseroles.

Chilli Powder

Warm with slight bite. Used in egg dishes, with baked beans, and in Mexican dishes.

Chives

A herb with delicate onion flavour. Used in salads, cheese dips, omelettes, with tomatoes and in soups.

Cinnamon

Sweet and spicy with a distinctive flavour. Used in buns, fruit cakes, ginger bread, milk puddings and apple pie.

Cloves

A strong spice. Used in puddings, apple pie, with baked ham, bread sauce, and ground in fruit cakes, buns and mince-meat.

Cumin Seed

Similar to caraway. Used in devilled dishes, in cheese dips, with minced beef, cabbage, sauerkraut and fish.

Curry Powder

Strong and spicy. Used in curries, sandwich fillings, stuffed eggs and savoury meat dishes.

Garlic Salt

Salt flavoured with garlic. May be used as a substitute for garlic for seasoning soups, stews etc.

Ginger

A hot rich spice. Used whole in pickles, chutney, ginger beer and wine. Ground in puddings, cakes, biscuits, ginger-bread, treacle tart, curries, and with Chinese dishes and melon.

Mace

Dried shell of the nutmeg. Has a fine flavour and can be used in sauces, marinades and stuffings.

Marjoram

A herb with a bitter but delicate flavour. Used with lamb, beef, veal, pork and poultry. With omelettes, fish, soufflés, stews, vegetables and salads.

Mint

A herb with a fresh piercing scent. Used in cooking new potatoes, peas, mint sauce, cream cheese, and sprinkled on tomatoes. Used in long refreshing drinks.

Mixed Spice

Aromatic blend of sweet spices. Used in cakes, biscuits, stewed fruit and puddings.

Nutmeg

Sweet, exotic and spicy. Used in doughnuts, custards, junkets and puddings. With ice-cream, stewed fruit, spicy cakes and cheese sauce.

Paprika

Mild, slightly sweet flavoured spice. Used in goulash, chicken in paprika sauce, egg and cheese dishes, canapés and rice dishes. Used also as a colourful garnish.

Parsley

Herb with a mild agreeable flavour and tremendous nutritional value. Used to sprinkle soups, stews, on rice and tomatoes, salads, minced meat, in parsley sauce, rissoles, savoury meat roll. Used as a garnish on sandwiches, and on meat and fish dishes.

Rosemary

Distinctive, delicate and sweetish flavour. Used to sprinkle over lamb before it is cooked, added to lamb stews and beef casseroles.

Sage

Strong, aromatic herb. Used with roast pork and for poultry stuffings.

Tarragon

Fresh, pleasant flavoured herb. Used with salads, chicken dishes, vinegar, fish and shell fish; in hollandaise, béarnaise and tartare sauces.

Thyme

Pungent and penetrating flavoured herb. Used in meat dishes, soups, bread stuffing with lemon, and in forcemeat, salads and tomatoes.

Turmeric

Clean mild flavoured spice. Used in pickles, relishes, salad dressings and to colour rice and curries.

Bouquet Garni

Three sprigs parsley, one sprig of thyme and a bay leaf tied together in a piece of muslin. Used in stews, casseroles, goulashes.

12-Miscellaneous Tips and Hints

Useful Amounts to Know

¼ lb. tea will make approx. 50 cups
1 pint of milk is needed for 50 cups
½ lb. sugar for 50 cups
1 quartern loaf will give 100 thin slices
½ lb. butter is required for 50 sandwiches
½ lb. sandwich spread for 50 sandwiches
1 quart ice-cream makes 12 servings.

Handy Measures

Syrup	1 tablespoon equals 1 oz.
Barbados sugar	1¼ tablespoons equal 1 oz.
Demerara sugar	1¼ tablespoons equal 1 oz.
Wholewheat flour	2 tablespoons equal 1 oz.
Grated cheese	4 tablespoons equal 1 oz.
Fresh breadcrumbs	1 cup equals 2½ oz.
Natural rice	1 cup equals 8 oz.
Rolled oats	1 cup equals 3¼ oz.
Gelatine	2 tablespoons equal 1 oz.

Gelatine

¼ oz. gelatine will set 1 pint whipped cream
½ oz. gelatine will set 1 pint white sauce
1 oz. gelatine will set 1 pint of clear liquid

Lemon Juice

Lemon juice added to fresh fruit salad helps to prevent fruit from discolouring. Mixed with mustard it keeps it moist.

Chocolate Cake

Always use chocolate and not cocoa powder if possible. If not possible then be sure to pre-cook cocoa in a little water before adding to cake mixture.

Fillets of Sole

Always cook fillets of sole just below boiling point so that they do not curl up like corkscrews.

Curdled Sauce

A little cold water added to a sauce about to curdle will save it.

Lemon Rind

Lemon rind kept in sugar canister gives delightful flavour to cakes and custards. Lemon rind in stews is delicious and so are lemon wedges with steaks.

Salty Soup

Soups in which ham or bacon bones are boiled will be less salty if a whole peeled potato is added when cooking and removed at the end of the cooking time.

Shiny Topped Buns

To give yeast buns a shiny top: dissolve a dessertspoon sugar in 1 tablespoon milk, bring to the boil, then brush this over each bun 10 minutes before the end of cooking time.

Home-made Yoghourt

Bring 1 pint of milk to the boil, remove from the heat and cool to lukewarm. Stir in 1 tablespoonful of plain yoghourt and mix well with a wooden spoon. Pour into well-washed yoghourt cups, and stand in heavy saucepan with lukewarm water up to $\frac{3}{4}$ of the cup. Cover and leave for 2 hours, topping up with hot water occasionally to keep the temperature lukewarm. Remove the cups and place in refrigerator for several hours.

Wholemeal Breadcrumbs

To make wholemeal breadcrumbs, put slices of stale bread on a baking sheet and cook in slow oven until brown and dry. Put through mincing machine and store in tight-lidded tin.

Fresh Lettuces

To keep lettuces fresh for several days, store in a large saucepan with airtight lid. To revive limp lettuce, remove old outer leaves and end of stalk, separate leaves, wash in cold water and leave in bowl of ice sprinkled with the juice of 1 lemon. A small piece of coal in the water helps to make the leaves crisp.

Coating with Egg and Breadcrumbs

For better results add 1 dessertspoon milk and 1 teaspoon vegetable oil for every egg used. Season well with salt and pepper.

Parsley

Use parsley as lavishly and as frequently as possible as it is rich in vitamin A and is also a source of iron.

Fresh Wholewheat Breadcrumbs

Wholewheat breadcrumbs quickly fried in hot butter with a little finely chopped chives or onions make an interesting topping for all kinds of dishes. Good with fried tomatoes, fried mushrooms or over cauliflower cheese.

Skimmed Milk

Dried skimmed milk is the cheapest form of improving the protein content of any dish. (2 lb. of dried milk to 1 gallon water gives a milk with twice the protein and calcium content of fresh milk at less than half the cost.)

INDEX

Index

Index